A PR

Five years ago something had happened in Gina's life which had turned her off men for good. She would never, never let one near her again, she vowed. Still, vows like that have been known to be broken. But if any man was ever going to break through the wall of Gina's reserve, it was certainly not going to be that infuriating, self-opinionated Mitch!

Another book you will enjoy
by KATE O'HARA

SUMMERHAZE

After five years working abroad, Romy had
returned happily to her home and family in
New Zealand—to face not only the hostility of
her sister Julie but the absolute contempt of
her father's farm manager, Quila Morgan.
What exactly had either of them got against
her?

A PRECIOUS THORN

BY

KATE O'HARA

MILLS & BOON LIMITED
15–16 BROOK'S MEWS
LONDON W1A 1DR

All the characters in this book have no existence outside the imagination of the Author, and have no relation whatsoever to anyone bearing the same name or names. They are not even distantly inspired by any individual known or unknown to the Author, and all the incidents are pure invention.

The text of this publication or any part thereof may not be reproduced or transmitted in any form or by any means, electronic or mechanical, including photocopying, recording, storage in an information retrieval system, or otherwise, without the written permission of the publisher.

This book is sold subject to the condition that it shall not, by way of trade or otherwise, be lent, resold, hired out or otherwise circulated without the prior consent of the publisher in any form of binding or cover other than that in which it is published and without a similar condition including this condition being imposed on the subsequent purchaser.

First published 1983
Australian copyright 1983
Philippine copyright 1983
This edition 1983

© Kate O'Hara 1983

ISBN 0 263 74305 5

Set in Monophoto Times 10 on 10 pt.
01–0883 – 66732

Made and printed in Great Britain by
Richard Clay (The Chaucer Press) Ltd,
Bungay, Suffolk

CHAPTER ONE

IT was late one Thursday afternoon nearing the middle of summer 1977 when Gina Wells experienced the encounter which was to change her life.

From where she stood gazing down from the louvred windows of her poky little office which overlooked the first floor of the large department store she could see Zac Hewson striding along the aisles, weaving his way through the throng of bustling shoppers made up mostly of office workers who had finished work at five o'clock and had only thirty short minutes in which to make their purchases before the shops closed for the day. Zac had a distinctive walk, Gina noted. Anyone who knew him would have had no difficulty in distinguishing him in a moving crowd. He loped along with long swinging jaunty strides which gave an observer the impression that he was taller than his five feet eight inches and that the balls of his feet were taking the burden of his weight. Yet even aside from his walk, he was someone you would notice and easily recognise again, for this was the situation he wanted to create and be in. Of this Gina was privately convinced. In fact she was willing to swear that he deliberately went all out to be a unique and not easily forgettable figure on the city's streets. For why else would he dress in the ostentatious fashions and colours he did, or change the colour of his hair every other week?

Gina disliked him with an intensity that was not too disproportionate – nor would it ever become disproportionate, for she had never allowed herself to feel anything extreme for a good five years and she didn't intend to allow this relative newcomer, bumptious and insolent as he was, to disrupt nor divert her from the pattern she had set herself and intended to faithfully follow for all the years that were to be allotted to her. Why she had assented to his appointment in the first place when one glance acquainted her with his affected indolent pose and one clash with his sardonic appraising stare was enough to confirm beyond doubt that 'here was trouble.'

'But he's extremely talented,' the store manager had protested when Gina had expressed reservations, and on this point Gina couldn't argue. Zac Hewson was indeed extremely talented, and his knowledge of his own talent and worth was something she suspected he had always realised, and if there ever had been an embryonic stage in its evolution she was willing to guarantee that it had emerged from that state fully matured.

'We're very lucky to be interviewing him at all,' said the store manager. 'The bigger centres would nab him without hesitation if he offered his services to them.'

And Gina had wished he would do just that. But no such luck, and she didn't need to rely on any such thing as woman's intuition to know why. The likes of Zac didn't come to be interviewed for the position of artist's assistant. They didn't go along with the theory of working one's way up the ladder. Lack of practical experience was no obstacle to be surmounted. It was the position of artist in Palmerston North's foremost department store that Zac was aiming for, and to usurp her from that position she knew was his intention and had been his intention from the very outset.

How could she have been such a fool! But thank heaven she had had the presence of mind to agree to his employment on certain conditions—the most important one being that she possess the irrevocable right to dismiss him if she deemed fit.

She was seated behind her cluttered desk when Zac appeared in the open doorway—dressed today in a less garish array of colours. At present his hair was black and sitting all over his head in a mass of upright spikes. Gina couldn't truthfully say even to herself that he looked ridiculous, because she simply couldn't imagine him looking any other way. He wore a loose-fitting lemon shirt beneath braces that held up equally loose-fitting grey trousers. On his feet were the inevitable white sandshoes, always startling clean and bright. Adorning the lobe of one ear was an array of gold studs.

Gina looked up from her work and wasn't surprised to discover that Zac had taken it upon himself to enter her office and sit down in the chair before her desk. He had one leg bent so that his ankle could rest over the knee of the other. Long slim hands were folded loosely across his lap and the front legs of the chair were lifted from their contact with the floor as he tilted the chair back.

'You wanted to see me?' he asked.

His pale face was expressionless and yet he managed to exude insolence from every pore. Gina felt every emotion in her rush headlong into one all-consuming desire to rise, reach over and slap his face, hard!

She sat there, however, very still, willing her face into a blank mask. This was no good. The realisation wasn't a new one, but still it pounced on her with a startling vivid clarity revealing even more definitely that which she had always suspected. Zac Hewson was young, but he was no fool. His characteristics and mode of dress weren't adopted because he could find no other way in which to express himself, or because he wanted to be different, nor were they contrived in order to shock or as a means by which to portray his rejection of all that was considered average, acceptable and normal by the majority of those in society. A sudden sharp stab of insight told Gina that here was a person who wanted to be noticed by all and his talents extolled by all, but even as this craving was being satisfied he laughed at those who noticed and extolled him, because he knew that the real Zac Hewson was kept a very close secret.

Gina couldn't entirely suppress a shiver that rippled through her. Could she be as clever as she knew Zac Hewson to be? Were her wits as acute as his? She could only hope so.

'Yes, I wanted to see you,' she began coolly, not flinching as she would liked to have done from the secretive smile lurking in his pale blue eyes. 'I thought I stipulated that you were to dress the cosmetics window in grey and pink. At lunchtime I couldn't help but notice that you'd disregarded my instructions.'

'Yes.'

'Would you care to elaborate beyond a monosyllabic answer?'

He lifted his shoulders in a bored, urbane fashion. 'To my mind, black and crimson are pink and grey, but a less—frustrated, shall we say—form.'

Gina steeled herself and forced her response to be bland and smooth-flowing. 'This is not the first instruction I've given that you've flagrantly disregarded.'

He sighed, indicating faint regret. 'You're right, of course. I guess it's my nature at fault, really. It rebels at repression but exults when it's allowed to express freedom. It can't abide where there's joylessness, so I guess it gets the better of me and takes over.'

It cost her a great deal of self-control not to betray any sign that she did in fact understand the nuances in all that he said. She looked at him impassively. 'If joy is the only expression you're able to create through your work, then it would seem that your talents as an artist are very limited. What about peace and serenity?'

'We're displaying cosmetics, aren't we? Not baby wear—or corsetry for the matronly or spinsterish.'

Gina continued calmly to hold the pale stare that was now blatantly mocking her. 'When you re-dress that window tomorrow morning, in accordance with my former instructions, take time out to make a study of the product you're displaying. You will note that the cosmetics are aimed at a certain market which, for once, does not incorporate the young.' Gina lowered her gaze to the sheet of paper that lay before her on the desk and set her signature to it—but not before witnessing the slight diminishing effect her revelation had upon his self-assurance. Carefully she folded the paper and slipped it into a brown envelope.

'That display is good, excellent in fact, and you know it. I suggest that if anything is to be changed it should be the product.'

'The product stays. The dressings go.' Gina licked the flap and sealed the envelope.

'What if I refuse?' Zac sneered silkily. 'What will you do? Arrange to have me fired.'

Right then, Gina would have given a great deal not to have had to look up and into the unpleasant countenance of her new assistant, but like all distasteful tasks in life, they had to be tackled sooner or later. And the sooner this cocky young upstart was taught his place the better off she'd be. She looked at him directly and dispassionately. '*I'm* not firing you,' she told him with subtle emphasis. 'You're very talented, but in your anxiety and haste to display your talents and ambitions, the young tend to be a little careless and a mite too obvious.' Gina rose to her feet and slipped the strap of her bag over her shoulder. 'I've put in for a raise for you,' she went on, and reaching for the sealed envelope, she lifted it, waved it briefly and tossed it into the out-tray. 'I'm sure that, like me, the store would wish to convey how highly they regard your talents.' And lifting her bag of groceries from the corner of her desk, she crossed to the door and waited expectantly for Zac to rise to his feet and proceed through before her. Which he did finally in something of a daze.

After he had gone, Gina experienced the overwhelming desire to collapse into the chair he had just vacated and remain there until the trembling in her body ceased. But such weakness, and the reason for it, angered her. She pulled the door to until it gave a sharp click, then made her way briskly towards the escalator.

Her first face-to-face combat with Zac Hewson and she had won! She had outmanoeuvred him by reacting unpredictably to his attempts to assert himself and nullify her authority over him. But it was a dubious victory and she wondered, as she made her way through the emptying store to the front doors, if he had any idea just how deeply his barbs had cut into her. Frustrated, repressed, spinsterish—they hadn't been words that had simply sprung to his tongue. No, they had been carefully chosen. Young, she had called him, but she too had chosen her words and had used that term in an effort to minimise him and any importance that she might be tempted to attach to his ploys. At twenty-four he was three years younger than she; however, she suspected that when dealing with an entity such as Zac Hewson, years had no relevance.

So preoccupied had she become, Gina was only vaguely aware of the heat of the outdoors rising to envelop her and totally oblivious of the people around her. When someone cannoned into her, the sudden violence catapulted her back into reality. Automatically her arms went out to save herself and the sack of groceries crashed on to the mosaic tiling which lay situated between the middle and side windows of the shop and its entrance and the pavement.

Gina gazed down in dismay while the man with whom she had collided had crouched and was gathering up the scattered items. Recovering finally, she crouched also and began to help him return the groceries to their bag.

'Can't do much about rescuing those peanuts,' the man was saying, and Gina noticed absently that there was a drawl to his voice.

'It doesn't matter,' she assured him, feeling the peanuts that escaped from the confines of their packet crunching beneath her feet.

'That's about all, I think,' said the stranger, straightening and lifting the groceries without effort.

Gina rose also and looked into his face and met a pair of blue eyes that were regarding her as though they had been granted a pleasant surprise. Becoming a trifle more flustered than she was already, she brushed back a strand of hair that had escaped from a style that was caught back severely from her face, and made too relieve him of the bag. 'I'm sorry for walking into you like that. I wasn't watching where I was going.'

'I can assure you that I don't mind in the least,' he said in a slow heartfelt way, his appreciative yet smiling blue eyes resting with disconcerting directness on her face. 'May I carry these for you? Have you a car?'

'Yes, yes, I have ...' Then, as she was about to assure him that she could manage perfectly well and escape the stare which she was beginning to find somewhat offensive, she caught sight of the familiar black head and the unmistakable swagger of Zac heading along the street towards them. Assailed by a rashness quite contrary to her nature, she allotted the stranger her full attention.

'Well, actually that would be very helpful of you,' she said. 'The bag doesn't look as strong as it was. My car is in a park only a few minutes' walk from here.' And together they turned in the direction from which Zac was coming. 'You're not from around here, are you?' she asked him, looking up at him in an endeavour to appear to the passing Zac as though she was deeply engrossed in conversation with this man who was her companion.

Let's hope this will give him cause to be confused! she was thinking to herself, and teach him not to believe all that he hears from the store's gossip-mongers. Not that they were lying when they discussed her, she knew. She was a loner. She preferred to be alone and she didn't date and had certainly never become involved with any male member of Illingworth's staff since the commencement of her employment with them five years previously, and she had no intention of changing the stance she had taken in this respect. She grinned to herself with a marked absence of amusement. 'I wonder what they'll make out of this when Zac reveals that he's seen the "ice-artist" strolling along the street with a man—a man who was carrying her groceries, what's more?' She almost laughed aloud.

'This is my car here. Thank you for bearing my burden,' she smiled rather briefly at the man and reached inside her shoulder bag for her keys.

'If you'd come out and have a meal with me tomorrow evening, I would consider myself handsomely rewarded.'

The invitation took her completely aback and she looked at him seriously then for the first time. She saw a man who, probably because of his size and the nature of his build, looked shorter than he was. However, standing alongside him she was forced to accept that he was possibly a good four to five inches taller than her five feet seven inches. Clad as he was in slacks and a

patterned, short-sleeved open-necked shirt, enough of
his physique was displayed to give Gina the impression
that he had a firm well-muscled body that was as hard
as rock. He looked hard and as though he'd lived hard.
The thought flashed through her mind, startling her.
She doubted that she had ever met, much less
associated with, a man who had lived hard, so on what
basis she had formed that assumption she couldn't say.
Perhaps her instincts hadn't shrivelled up and died from
lack of practise after all. Her gaze flickered over the
dark close-cropped hair, free from threads of grey even
though she judged him to be in his mid to late thirties,
the wide smile and audacious blue eyes which were
looking at her so directly beneath rather heavy brows.
She felt herself withdraw and everything in her shrink
and curl up. Very very rarely was it that she met a man
for whom she could feel even the slightest rapport or
attraction. But never before could she remember having
been so strongly or sufficiently put off to say to herself
quite unequivocally: 'Definitely not my type—at all!'

'No. Thank you, but I couldn't do that.' A slight
nebulous smile came and went and she turned away
from the sight of him, his deeply lined rather
pugnacious face which bespoke a life and a wealth of
experience Gina preferred not to be confronted with,
and fitted the key into the lock of her blue Corolla.

'Why couldn't you? Aren't you free?'

'Yes, but . . .'

'Well then, could you not have pity on a lonely
stranger in your country? I've heard all about how
friendly and hospitable you people are supposed to be.
I'd certainly appreciate the opportunity to experience it
for myself.'

'I'm sure,' Gina's response came clipped. 'But I'm
sorry, I'm just not the flag-waving type.' She reached
for and relieved him of the sack of groceries and bent
and deposited them on the front passenger seat of her
car.

'There's room for change in all of us, they say.
Personally, I find changes exciting.'

Gina straightened and once more turned to face him

and was in time to see his gaze lifting up from the direction of her legs and hips. 'I don't,' she said pointedly. She extended him another smile, suspect and pseudo-apologetic. 'Thank you again.' She slid in behind the wheel, but was precluded from closing the door when he leaned forward, draping one crooked arm over the roof of the car and the other over the top of the open door.

Chagrined, she shot him a haughty stare. 'Do you mind. . . .?'

But he ignored her as she began to upbraid him. 'I'll pick you up at seven-thirty tomorrow night,' he cut in with a quiet bold insistence that told her he was very accustomed to getting his own way. And what caused her to bridle afresh was the insidious way he was using his stronger will and manipulative nature to subjugate her own. The nerve of the man!

'I think it's only fair to tell you that I harbour an especially strong antipathy for brash, overbearing . . .' She stopped. What on earth had he said he was? Australian, American, Canadian? She hadn't listened to a word he'd uttered during their short walk to the car. She groaned inwardly. How *could* she have been so stupid?

'American,' he supplied helpfully, his blue eyes twinkling. 'I'm American.'

'Goodbye, Mr . . .'

'Mitchell. J.P.'

Gina's lips compressed into a tight line and she tugged hard at the handle of the door, but it didn't budge and he appeared to have not the slightest intention of removing his bulk from the aperture. She returned her hand to the wheel and stared silently, stonily ahead of her.

'Where can I pick you up?'

'I prove appalling company.'

'That I've suspected, but *I* have to own to harbouring a strong penchant for blondes with grey-green eyes.'

Irritated now to the very boundaries of her endurance, Gina felt sorely tempted to start the car and stamp her foot down hard on the accelerator.

Managing to curb this impulse, she came finally to accept that there was only one way out of this predicament. Unclenching her teeth, she threw a smile up at him, bright and sweet this time but as equally false as its predecessors, and acquiesced. 'Well, why not? But I'd rather not go for a meal, if you don't mind. Friday being the end of the week and late night, it's the only time I get to shop. Let's say I meet you outside Illingsworth store at eight-thirty.'

'Do you usually arrange not to be called for by your escorts?'

'No—but then I usually don't allow myself to be picked up by strangers either. So there you are, two changes I've made in my life this evening. You should be pleased.'

'I will be—if we manage to couple the changes with a little excitement.' The man grinned at her in a way that told her he not only had his doubts about that, but that he knew only too well the workings of her mind. He stepped back and closed the door while she clipped her seatbelt into place and started the car.

'What a boor!' she exclaimed to herself as she drove swiftly out of the car-park and shot out on to a road which was fortunately free of traffic. So obvious. So typically male, egotistical and predatory. Not so stupid, though, that he didn't guess that she had no intention of meeting him at eight-thirty tomorrow or at any time, anywhere. As if she'd allow herself to be picked up by anyone, much less a crass and cocky coarse stranger to her city and country who was patently at a loose end and on the lookout for a diversion. And to strike up a casual liaison with a personable female the second an opportunity to do so should present itself would prove a very agreeable diversion indeed. Gina shuddered. No, thank *you*!

Pushing the incident far from her mind, she relaxed behind the wheel and enjoyed the feel of the summer breeze and the late afternoon sun settling hotly over the bare arm nearest to the window. How she loved the warmer months! During the spring, the city had had a fresh, dewy look about it. The many trees in the city's

seventeen-acre square and those lining the streets had
adorned themselves in garments of bright green which
had darkened in colour as summer approached. The air
which had then been soft, clear and fragrant was now
shimmering with a hot dry haze and inclined to be
harsh and dusty. The grass in the parks and in the
public and private gardens was no longer green but
brown and no longer soft and plentiful but brittle and
sparse. And the mountain ranges which formed the
city's beautiful backdrop were forever changing. Gina
could never quite make up her mind when she most
liked the look of them, whether it was in the spring
when they rose in clear soft hues of green, blue and
mauve against the young blue sky, or whether it was in
summer when according to her imagination they
resembled a stage prop, a stark golden-brown cardboard
cut-out standing etched out before a brassy sky. This
was the stage they were coming to now and from which
an observer could gauge that summer was reaching its
peak. The sky was a relentless blue and the hills were
sharply defined and looked close enough to touch.
Though the vast areas of bush that covered the slopes
had wilted they would remain forever green, but the
fate of the usually lush pastures seemed inescapable as
each rainless day robbed them of more of their colour.

Gina pulled into the drive of her home, which was
situated on the corner of two quiet tree-lined streets.
The garage was one into which she drove straight from
the street and therefore there was no long driveway
taking up a substantial amount of her section. This was
only one of the features of the property which had
appealed to her when she had considered its purchase.
The house was a small two-bedroomed bungalow,
approximately fifty years old, with low bay windows,
well established gardens and a two-foot-high picket
fence encircling the front boundary of the section, and a
high coal-tar creosoted plank fence edging the back.
The mature trees and shrubs had almost decided Gina
before she had even viewed the interior of the house.
They had been so well tended over the years—
particularly the beautiful Japanese laurel and the

magnolia and silver birch in the front garden and the kowhai in the back. As she had inspected the inside of the house she had felt her heart leap within her, witnessing to her that this was the kind of house she would enjoy making into a home—her home.

Its potential had fired her artistic imagination and visions of minor alterations and entire colour schemes and furnishings had come crowding in on her. The front bedroom with its protruding corner windows and window seat and walk-in wardrobe had appealed to her immensely, and the first job she had tackled after moving in had been to paint the trimmings white and exchange the wallpaper of indecisive colour and pattern to one of a warm rich rose pink. The bathroom she was in the process of changing. The husband of her closest friend dealt with all the manual jobs she found herself unable to manage, such as the installing of a new shower tray and the stripping away of tiling, which she found cold and unappealing, from the walls and around the large old fashioned bath. The kitchen she had liked just as it was, with its two quarter-paned windows and quarter-paned french doors which led out on to a sheltered brick patio. To strip the walls and cupboards of their layers of paint in order that she could repaint them in the colours of her own choosing was a job she had reserved for wet weekends, but since there hadn't been any for several months she was fast finishing this onerous task in the evenings. Now that the laundry had been repositioned and the space successfully converted into a pantry, she knew a keen desire to see the kitchen in its completed state.

The dining-room and lounge were semi-combined, and this had been the only characteristic which Gina had had doubts about. She couldn't abide houses which had had walls knocked out in order to make two rooms into one, as had been done in this case. From the kitchen door one was able to see through the dining-room area into the lounge to where the widely curving bay window, complete with a fitted window seat, overlooked the front garden, shaded to some extent in the summer by the magnolia tree. However, since she had fully and creatively redecorated the entire area in colours of dull olive green for the walls and white for the trimmings and had installed carefully selected items of furniture, and had laid a shagpile carpet, she had grown to appreciate this feature of the house above all the others.

Many of her bits and pieces in the way of furniture, ornaments and pictures, she had acquired at auctions and garage sales, while the remainder, such as window dressings, cushions, rugs, paintings, pot hangers, were all examples of her own gifted handiwork. Her décor was a combination of old, such as her beautiful oak oval-shaped dining-room set, and new, such as the terracotta-coloured lounge suite, but she was proud of her achievements and considered she had transformed a house into a home that possessed both character and atmosphere.

Unlocking the back door, she slid the groceries on to the bench and walked through to the passage and into her bedroom, pulling her cotton smock off over her head as she went. Tossing it into the cane receptacle she had bought for such a purpose at the local market, she stepped out of her high-heeled sandals and then her skirt.

How good it felt to be able to pad around in any state of dress or undress in her own home without having to worry about encountering another human being. Such privacy was certainly a luxury, she thought, entering the shower box and revelling in the powerful jet of lukewarm water that cascaded over her perspiring skin. And it was one she had never once ceased to be thankful for throughout the three years she had been in possession of her own home. It had originally been her plan to redecorate and then advertise for someone to occupy the spare bedroom, but the renovations she had wanted to make were ones that took longer to eventuate in their final state in reality than they did to appear in her mind. Now she doubted very much if she could surrender even a little of the limitless freedom and independence she was enjoying. Also, since she had discovered that she didn't need company and in fact was only too glad to get home in the evenings, to the peace and quiet and solitude it provided where she could relax and do as she pleased, eat when she pleased and read, paint, sew or listen to music where and when she pleased, she realised that the prospect of changing her habits to make the provisions that would surely be required if someone should move in to share her accommodation with her was a very unpalatable one indeed.

She was becoming selfish, she admonished herself for the umpteenth time as, on a sudden impulse, she decided to wash her hair. She'd have to do something about the attitude she was allowing to creep into her life. But not yet. She couldn't face relinquishing the sense of serenity she had suffered a great deal to acquire. What did she care if people thought she was staid, holding herself aloof and allowing herself to become too introspective and too set in her ways? *They* obviously never had the capacity to be as deeply hurt as she had been ... No, it was silly, puerile to harp on along those lines. She had long since recovered from that particular tragedy in her life. After a prolonged period, the pain had been dulled and effectively quenched. But she was one who needed to be taught a lesson only once. Never again would she enter a situation as the naïve, trusting young girl she once had been. It was difficult to believe now that she actually had been so foolish.

Seated at her bedroom dressing table swathed in a navy towel and armed with a brush and blowdryer, she caught sight of the grim twist to her lips and realised with something of a shock that that was supposed to be a smile of self-satisfaction. Hastily she relaxed her facial muscles and affixed into place the cool composed mask that she had designed and perfected for herself and with which she had, years before, begun to purposely and religiously cloak her features. It flashed through her mind that such perfect expressionlessness was not exactly an improvement. In fact, if she were a stranger, male or female, and came face to face with Gina Wells, she didn't think she would like what she saw at all.

But what did it matter? She tossed her head and flicked the brush through her long straight dark ash-blonde hair. She had no desire to be first in the popularity stakes at work or anywhere else for that matter. When it came right down to it, and she was ruthlessly honest, she had to admit that she wasn't exactly crazy about herself. But who was ever that honest? It was extremely doubtful that anyone could claim to be one hundred per cent proud or satisfied with the image of their true selves which, from time to time, had the unpleasant knack of rising up to confront them.

Once her hair was dry and tied into a ponytail high on the back of her head, with the ends folded under and secured, Gina discarded the towel and dropped over her head a flowing full-length caftan, khaki in colour, with a scooped neckline and long, loose sleeves.

At work her colleagues saw her only with her hair up and clad in three-quarter-length smocks over jeans or skirts, and upon such evidence had obviously considered themselves justified in labelling her staid and spinsterish. However, in her tastes in everything from clothes to décor, she was anything but staid. Her wardrobe was full of clothes which she had designed and sewn and sometimes dyed and printed herself. However, since it was not often that she went out anywhere, opportunities to wear her more exquisite items of clothing were few and far between. More recently she had found an outlet for her creative talents and had begun designing clothes, scarves and fabric handbags for a small boutique, the owner of which was only too happy to buy from her all that she was able to offer. Of course time proved a very restrictive factor and the quantity she was able to produce was quite negligible. But one day she hoped to find herself in a position whereby she would be able to allot more time to what was now a hobby and less to her regular nine-to-five job.

After consuming a light meal of corned beef and salad, and icecream with fresh strawberries which were presently in abundance, Gina began her evening of

leisure by writing to her parents, who were owners of a
farm in the Hawkes Bay province, and spent the latter
stages of it poring over her sketchbook in an endeavour
to transfer ideas for a summer evening dress from her
mind on to paper.

CHAPTER TWO

THE following day, as she was on her way up to the
staff cafeteria to eat her lunch, Gina noticed that her
handling of the situation that had cropped up between
Zac Hewson and herself had been successful. The
cosmetics for the 'mature woman' were exquisitely
arranged amid colours of silver and dark shades of pink
and grey, and as she made a swift study of the display
she honestly doubted that she herself could have done
better.

It was at about that time that the events which had
followed yesterday afternoon's meeting with Zac
trembled on the brink of her memory, but they didn't
topple into it until a woman from the store's fashion
department came to occupy the same table as herself,
saying as she lit up a cigarette: 'That was some hunk of
a man I saw you with last night!'

Gina looked up somewhat blankly from the book she
was reading. 'Sorry . . .' Her voice faded as with a shock
she recalled the brash beefy American who had carried
her groceries to her car the night before. She tried not
to grimace as she spoke noncommittally: 'Did you
think so?'

'I'd probably be locked up if I told you what I really
thought!' Maida laughed throatily. 'But I would've
hardly guessed he'd have been the sort to attract you.'

Gina tried to keep distaste from leaking into her
features as she studied the other woman, less than ten
years her senior, always perfectly made up and
immaculately groomed. A good-time woman, a man's
woman, married but forever on the lookout for a

flirtatious encounter with any male member of the store's staff, irrespective of age or marital status. Yes, you're dead right, Gina told her silently. He's definitely not my sort, but I wouldn't mind betting that you're thinking—and I agree with you—that he's certainly yours.

'Oh?' she spoke aloud and with vague interest. 'And what makes you think so?'

'Well,' Maida shrugged, her lips twitching as though she was struggling to suppress her mirth at some private musings of her own, 'he looked too red-blooded for an innocent like you to handle, if you know what I mean.'

'No,' Gina lied coolly, 'as a matter of fact, I don't know what you mean.'

'Well, my dear,' Maida drew on her cigarette once more and then extinguished it and with the same fingers she had used to press out the cigarette, she patted Gina's bare arm, 'you have a think about it. I'm sure you'll work it out.' And with a secretive smile, which Gina found as objectionable as the woman's touch on her arm, Maida rose to her feet. 'I suppose you see him regularly?'

Gina looked up at her and hated having to do so. 'Every opportunity.'

Maida gave another throaty laugh which covered a multitude of allusions. 'My, my, you are a dark horse, aren't you?' Her gaze became mildly speculative. 'Still, I don't blame you. If I were you, I wouldn't let him out of my sight. But if ever the day should dawn when you find him a mite too . . .' she paused deliberately, '. . . demanding, shall we say, don't let him go without giving me an introduction, will you?'

Gina returned her smile with one that was every bit affected as hers was. Awful, obnoxious woman! she exclaimed to herself as she watched the impeccable figure glide away towards easier more profitable prey. And she shuddered and wondered who else had seen her in that short space of time she had spent in the American's company. Still, it was interesting to discover that Maida found him attractive. Yes, to learn another woman's opinion was very enlightening indeed. Even if that woman did happen to be Maida Berry who, it seemed, had developed the capacity to find all men attractive without exception. But her own intuition told her that Maida would never have approached her and said such things if she hadn't been genuinely and sufficiently impressed by the sight of the American. Like attracted like, she thought spitefully, still smarting from the remark the woman had made and at which she had taken immediate offence: 'He looked too red-blooded for an innocent like you to handle.' There had been a slight but significant pause before the word 'innocent' and Gina recognised only too clearly the inference the woman had placed upon it. Ice-artist was a nickname she had been assigned, when and by whom she had no idea, nor did she have any desire to find out, but nonetheless she didn't waste time entertaining false hopes that gossip about her was confined only to a small group. As far as she was concerned all, whether interested or not, would have learned her nickname. In effect, what Maida had been intending to express was her amazement that such a red-blooded male should want to associate with a cold, lacklustre personality such as herself.

Good grief! Unable to concentrate any longer on her book, Gina slammed it shut. In her opinion, a girl would have to be either crazy or positively desperate to desire to go out with a man like J. P. Mitchell. He was all brawn, with as much subtlety as a steamroller, wasn't he? She almost laughed as she returned to her office and workroom. She couldn't even remember what he looked like, except that he was big and had too many teeth—as did most Americans. She shrugged and returned early to her work, only to find that her unpleasant encounter with Maida Berry wouldn't leave her mind.

By the time she had arrived home from work that evening, she had decided to meet the American as she had arranged. Something inside her head insisted that this was an action she was going to regret, while something else kept niggling at her, challenging her. What had Maida seen in him that had completely eluded her?

If anything at all! a voice in her head scoffed. The woman in her was dead, the cool clear decisive voice went on. That was what she wanted, wasn't it? That was what she had worked at all these years to achieve. Why risk losing all the fruits of her hard labour?

'I won't lose anything at all,' she argued aloud with total conviction. 'That stupid woman would find Harold Steptoe an attractive proposition! I'm just going to prove to myself that I'm cool and level-headed but not inordinately unconscious of a genuinely attractive man. And since I'm already sure that this man would have to be one of the least attractive men I've run across for a long time, I intend to prove it. Surely there's no danger in that.'

Gina changed from her work clothes into an attractive lemon-coloured dress with a skirt that flared and flounced at the hem and a scoop-necked bodice, attractively pintucked and supported by narrow shoulder straps. She restyled her hair, catching it into a chignon at the nape of her neck. She had no wish to appear to this man as though she had gone to a lot of trouble in her preparations, nevertheless her own sense of pride would not allow her to go out anywhere looking less than her best. With a disciplined effort, she managed to apply her make-up with a hand more restricted than usual and decided against wearing any form of jewellery aside from her wristwatch.

At eight o'clock she set out for town on foot. Except for those days on which she genuinely intended to shop, she always walked to work. It took her fifteen to twenty minutes when she was wearing flat-heeled sandals; however, because tonight she had chosen to wear a high-heeled wedge-soled pair, she elected to give herself more time so that she could walk leisurely and enjoy the beauty of the young balmy evening.

The sun, though it hadn't set, was lost to sight to her and the remnants that could be seen through the variety of trees that lined the avenue were in the form of golden rays which were extending up and outward to touch the smattering of high cloud, painting them ever deepening shades of peach and apricot. Since arriving in and making Palmerston her home, Gina had discovered that the sunsets in the area were often pretty and even spectacular. The sun wasn't as plentiful nor the heat as intense as in Hawkes Bay, but Gina hadn't minded this. What she did find a less attractive feature of her adopted city was the often persistent winds, even if they did help to keep the district pollution-free as the residents claimed. However, not even a breeze whispered through the leafy canopies under which she passed that evening, and as she strolled, she managed to shed in some measure the apprehension which had steadily mounted in her from the moment the decision to keep this date had been made. There was, of course, the distinct possibility that he might not turn up, and she latched on to this hope, extracting from it a certain penurious comfort.

She wasn't to be so lucky. Just as she drew level with the particular entrance to the shop where their collision had taken place, her gaze, which she allowed to wander in an outward display of nonchalance, alighted on a figure approaching with long confident strides across one of several of the square's areas of withered grass, beneath the trees and on across the road towards where she stood. As she watched him she felt her heart plummet with dismay. Her mouth went suddenly dry while conversely her palms became moist. She wanted desperately to turn and flee, but she had left it much too late to escape, and besides, it seemed that her feet were rooted to the spot.

She groaned inwardly as she took in his pugnacious, peculiarly ugly face, grinning at her in a manner that she could only describe as gloating. 'I must be mad!' she cried silently as everything within her revolted at having to tolerate even for a second the overbearing, overpowering presence of this man. Whatever it was that emanated from him had, she was positive, doubled in strength since she had last been subjected to it, and she felt sure it would suffocate her within the space of a half an hour at least. Oh, how could she have been such a dolt as to listen to someone like Maida Berry when one very pertinent experience in her life had already taught her how imperative it was for one to develop reliable instincts? What was the point of developing them if she wasn't going to heed them?

'Hi!' he greeted her with hearty enthusiasm, his face wreathed in smiles, all genuine and all somehow boyish and frankly triumphant. 'It's good to see you!'

In comparison, Gina's responding smile was wan and lukewarm, but he appeared not to notice, and she decided that it was a good thing that he was so effusive, for the supply in him would more than make up for the lack of it in her.

'I did wonder whether you'd show,' he went on. 'When you drove off last night, I must admit I had my doubts.'

'You did?' Gina replied, not without sarcasm. 'I can't think why.'

'Now that you're here, neither can I,' he said unbelievably.

Gina shot him a searching sideways glance. He had missed the innuendo in her remark, that she was willing to swear. She had heard of the characteristic naïveté of Americans, surely she hadn't come into contact with such a one ...

'But you drove off in such a hurry, I didn't get your name.'

'Gina,' she told him briefly. 'And yours?'

'Mitchell, J.P. Didn't I tell you?'

'You did, but I can hardly call you J.P., can I?'

'Why not? I'm called that—among other things.' And when warm infectious laughter followed this obvious comment, Gina at last discovered something to like in this man whose quantity of energy and conviviality she found excessive.

'J.P.,' she repeated to herself. 'J.P. Justice of the Peace. No, I can't call you ...'

'Justice of the what?'

Gina sighed. 'Never mind, just tell me what J.P. stands for.'

'Joseph Parron.'

'Then may I call you Joseph?'

The man shrugged his well-muscled shoulders. 'If it'll

make you happy—why not? Or call me Mitch, as do most of my friends. Now is there anywhere you'd specifically like to go?' His blue eyes were twinkling at her with a mixture of both merriment and appreciation, neither of which Gina felt she could withstand. She looked away and stifled a sigh of hopelessness. The only place she had any desire to go was home, and alone.

'No, I have no particular preference.' Her apathetic response would have been enough to put to death the enthusiasm of the average man, but Gina had come to suspect that Joseph Parron Mitchell was not the type one would term as average in any circumstances.

'In that case I have a friend who might welcome a little company. I think he said he's going along to a hotel called the Coachman. Do you know it?'

Gina looked at him aghast. 'I've heard of it,' she told him distantly. Surely he wasn't suggesting that she accompany him to a *bar*?

'Is it not a very reputable place?' he asked, for once correctly interpreting her response.

'I wouldn't know. I'm not in the habit of frequenting such places.'

'Well, let's look at it this way: it'll be a new experience for both of us.'

Gina looked at him, making no attempt to conceal her scepticism. 'Are you asking me to believe that you don't go to hotels?'

'No, in my line to avoid them is practically an impossibility. What I'm trying to say is that if you haven't been to the Coachman before, and I certainly haven't, it will be a novel experience for both of us.'

'Hmm, more novel for some than for others.' She compressed her lips even more firmly than before. 'Very well, but I trust it will be the lounge bar that we'll patronise.'

'Most definitely the lounge bar,' he replied readily and with such unexpected seriousness that Gina turned her head swiftly to look at him. Her suspicions were well founded and she discovered him observing her with a distinct mischievous gleam in his bright blue eyes. She stiffened.

'You're a rather prim sort, aren't you?' And there was a soft chuckle in his voice.

A gentle tide of heat crept up from her neck into her cheeks, and the experience was so unaccustomed, she didn't quite know how to react. As they were crossing the road, he stopped in the middle on the island lined with saplings and lit up a cigarette, while Gina thankfully carried on to the other side, all the while wishing fervently that the brief respite from his company could be prolonged permanently.

'What is your line?' she asked in an endeavour to make the best of the situation in which she had so stupidly landed herself. They were traversing the near deserted Square and she found herself having to shorten her step, for Mitch now seemed disinclined to walk with the same swinging rapid strides with which he had approached her. And while he appeared to be enjoying his leisurely stroll through the beautiful, carefully tended gardens, their pace did by no means suit Gina. To her it suggested intimacy and, no matter how casual, intimacy and friendship were some things that could never rise up between herself and the likes of him. She flexed the fingers of one hand in agitation.

'I'm in the Army,' came his reply, and Gina didn't know whether it was accidental or whether it was the enormity of his reply which caused her foot to slip off the side of her strapless sandal. She stumbled, but before she fell his hard warm hands had shot out to catch her, one grasping her upper arm while the other formed a clamp of steel on the soft indentation that was her waist. Gina winced a little and wondered if he was conscious of just how strong his grip was. As soon as she was upright and steady, his hands left her and only warm imprints remained in place of where they had been.

'Are you okay?' he asked.

'Yes—yes, thank you. I often go over on my ankle like that. It's just as well I'm not partial to very high heels.' She knew she was babbling and could only hope that she was not being too inarticulate, while in her mind his reply was echoing and re-echoing relentlessly.

'My God!' she was horrified. 'The *Army!*' Well, she really had made a colossal blunder. No further confirmation was needed on that score! Surely there was something funny to be found somewhere in all this. But if there was she certainly couldn't see it yet. Perhaps she would one day in the future, when this disastrous evening was far behind her.

'Are you out here on a visit?' she asked stiltedly.

'Uh-huh. From Schofield in Honolulu.'

'Oh.'

'There's a company of us out here. Have you heard of Schofield?'

'I suppose I must have, since the name doesn't seem totally unfamiliar, but I know about as much about Schofield Camp in Hawaii as I do about Linton Camp in Palmerston North—and that's precisely nothing.'

'Schofield Barracks,' he corrected her without emphasis, and went on: 'That's unusual, isn't it? I would have thought the local girls here would have met up with Army fellers at some time or another.'

Gina shrugged in an aloof fashion. 'Maybe they do, I wouldn't know.'

'Not you, huh?'

'I'm not a exactly a "local girl",' she informed him. 'I didn't grow up here.' He was silent.

'You're an officer, I suppose?' She tried to keep the thread of 'last hope' out of her voice.

When the silence continued and he didn't reply immediately, Gina turned her head to look at him. He was drawing on his cigarette and paused to look at her briefly, narrowing his gaze against the rise of smoke before lowering them to watch as he carefully pressed out the butt and dropped it into the nearby rubbish bin. She fancied she saw his lips twist in a brief rather self-deprecating smile before his eyes lifted to rest on hers, and the unexpected humourless quality of their expression chilled her and the slight equally humourless grin evoked a sudden nervous sensation within her. Why did she get the peculiar feeling that her question hadn't exactly been unexpected, but had nonetheless disappointed him, and the fact that this should actually bother her made her impatient. She turned away. She had her answer, and either way it would have made no difference to her.

'I'm a Top Sergeant—a disappointment to you, maybe.'

'I had no expectations, so I'm not disappointed.' And in this Gina spoke the truth. 'I was making an assumption, I suppose, going solely by your age. I don't know anything about the forces or how they operate.' And by her tone she ensured that she conveyed to him that she had no urge to be educated.

As they entered the lounge bar of the Coachman a wave of even deeper dismay broke over her. She hated crowds, smoke and noise, and here it seemed she was to be thrust into the midst of all three. As she gazed about her helplessly, she felt a touch on her arm and Mitch drew her outside into the foyer. 'Wait here a minute and I'll go in and see if I can find Lou. We might find somewhere quieter to have a drink.' His bulky frame disappeared through the crowds and it was only when, through the glass door, she caught sight of him returning that she realised that had he stayed away a few seconds longer, she would have recognised that this was an ideal opportunity to escape. Unfortunately, the thought occurred to her too late, and she wanted to kick herself as she watched Mitch push through the door followed by a dark-haired girl who was almost as tall as Mitch himself and an inch or so taller than the man who preceded her.

'Gina, I'd like you to meet a pal of mine, Lou de Laney, and this is his friend, Pamela Ansell.'

Lou and Pamela greeted her with an exuberance that caused her own acknowledgment of their introduction to appear cool and constrained. Which it was, for she felt about as drawn to them as she did to Mitch. She sighed to herself. What an awkward, uncomfortable evening this promised to be!

'Lou and Pam suggest we go to the bar upstairs,' Mitch was saying. 'It's probably quite crowded, but it will be quieter and there's no band music—only a piano, I've been told. Does that appeal to you?'

Gina looked at him and fixed a smile on her face. 'Why not?' she said, and taking a few rapid side steps, she managed to avoid the touch of his hand at her elbow and mounted the stairs unaided.

In the upstairs bar they found an alcove which faced on to the small dance floor at the edge of which a pianist was playing a bracket of popular numbers. The two men stood back to allow Pam and herself to slide into the seats before them, and Gina did so with great inward reluctance. Mitch slipped in beside her and immediately she felt trapped by his bulk. The heavy weight of his thigh was thrust alongside her own and she recoiled instantly from the contact with such foreign hardness and warmth. She felt him shoot a glance at her while at the same time moving away from her as if to give her more room.

She sat there very still, frozen, rigid and unable to relax, listening to the ribaldry going on between Pam and Lou, the uproarious laughter among the three of them and the conversation between the two men, speaking herself only when spoken to. Lou was also an American, she quickly gathered, a smaller man than Mitch, and handsome in the conventional sense, and he struck her as being more brash and egotistical than she already considered Mitch to be. Not that Pam seemed to be in the same dilemma as she was in or to be suffering from the same misgivings. In fact she was thoroughly enjoying the line Lou was handing her and the 'Army' stories being exchanged between the two men, and, as it was soon revealed, she was more than able and willing to compete with them when it came to telling jokes. She was an attractive girl of about twenty-five, by no means innocent or naïve, and seemed, to Gina, to be free of all inhibitions and totally lacking in discretion. Her whole restless, ever-buoyant personality suggested that she was all out for a good time and would look at anyone whom she considered could and would give it to her.

A pick-up. A girl whom Lou had chatted up in the bar downstairs some time before she and Mitch arrived ... And her thoughts came to an abrupt halt as she realised that if this girl was a pick-up, what did that make her? If it had been possible for her to withdraw even further away from Mitch she would have done so that very instant, but the imprisoning alcove wall formed an unyielding barricade. She had allowed herself to be picked up, for the first time in her life, and by a foreigner, a man in the Army, which was worse— who was not even an officer! How could she have been so abysmally stupid? she asked herself yet again, and was washed in a tide of self-loathing. Well, it served her right, she told herself bitterly. This was a lesson that would teach her to stay true to the path she had first set herself, five years before. In the meantime she would suffer this nightmare and see it through with as much dignity as she could muster. And so she sat, silent for the most part, with her hands folded on her lap and with her gin squash sitting, virtually untouched, on the table in front of her.

'Would you like to dance?' Mitch asked her suddenly. He had turned some time ago and had sat looking at her in silence ever since. The one time she had gathered enough courage to glance quickly furtively at him and then away had given her no hint as to what he might be thinking.

'No—thank you.' A polite smile came and went and again she found she couldn't withstand the direct quality of his stare and so averted her gaze. 'I like to watch,' she murmured.

At that moment Lou rose and pulled Pam up from her seat, but all the while his eyes were trained on Gina. As if in response to some invisible pull she casually glanced up at him and as she met his gaze, outwardly jocular and teasing, something in her registered that there was yet another quality present in his eyes and the sudden discovery that this man did not like her, even slightly, pierced right through her. So taken aback was she, she could only sit there dumbstruck as he delivered to her an ultimatum underscored with an implication that reached, as it was meant to, her ears only. 'If you're not up dancing by the time we get back,' he said, 'you'll dance with me, and I warn you—I don't take no for an answer.'

'That's what I like,' Pam crooned, draping a crooked arm on his shoulder, 'a masterful man!' And he swept her off on to the dance floor where they swiftly mingled with other dancers and became lost to sight.

Even before she was aware of it, Gina was on her feet. Mitch looked at her enquiringly. 'Well, you heard your friend,' she forced herself to say lightly. 'I think I'd rather dance a foxtrot with you than a tango with him.'

Mitch grinned and stood up. 'He sure is energetic, isn't he? He's got powerful drive and the strength of two men twice his size.'

Gina gave a perfunctory noncommittal smile and looked away over his shoulder as his arm encircled her. She held herself ramrod-stiff and each time she made a concerted effort to relax, she began to tremble. She hadn't been in a man's arms for over five years, and never in ones that seemed capable of such strength, nor felt beneath her hands flesh so hard. Far from being excited by such features, she was frankly repulsed, and it took every ounce of self-control to prevent herself from jerking away from him. Lou was not the only one who exuded excessive power and drive, she found herself thinking. They both owned tremendous magnetic vitality which they used to manipulate and mesmerise, and whereas Lou's was wiry and overt, in comparison Mitch's was quiet, latent, controlled but working for him unceasingly. They were like a pair of powerful healthy animals, and the simile caused her revulsion to manifest itself in a long deep shudder which rippled through her and she was by that time uncaring of how Mitch should interpret the alternate quaking and stiffening and straining away of her body.

When silently he shepherded her back to their table, he didn't step back this time to allow her to be seated before him. Instead he slipped in first and instinctively, Gina guessed that he had been aware, possibly from the outset, of her aversion to all form of contact with him.

Finally it was time to leave, and Gina managed in time to resist the urge to leap to her feet when Pam suggested to her that they go and comb their hair.

Instead, she rose leisurely and followed her out of the bar and along a carpeted dimly lit corridor to where an illuminated sign overhung the ladies' room.

She gave her a reflection a cursory glance in the mirror as she washed her hot sticky hands beneath the cold tap. Drying them quickly, she left Pam brushing her hair and went on down the stairs to the foyer where the men had said they would meet them. The opportunity at last had come to put distance between her and the ghastly atmosphere of this hotel, and soon there would be an even greater distance inserted between her and J. P. Mitchell, and this thought lent buoyancy to her steps.

She had almost reached the bottom of the staircase when she was checked by the sound of drawling male voices which came from immediately beyond the corner of the staircase and drifted clearly to her.

'You sure managed to strike a dud there, didn't you, old buddy?'

'What are you on about?'

'You know what I'm on about. That dame Gina.'

'She's got a sexy mouth,' came Mitch's calm reply.

'*What?* You're kidding! She's got a mouth like a compressed paper clip. Man, what were you thinking about when you picked her up?'

'She has class.'

Lou uttered a smothered expletive and snorted: 'Class ain't gonna keep you warm at night.'

'When I want to be kept warm at night, I know just where to go, Lou. Sometimes, believe it or not, I simply like to talk with a woman.'

Lou gave a hoot of delighted laughter. Then: 'She doesn't even do much of that either. Come on, buddy, admit it—you picked a dud. Or perhaps you're losing your touch . . .'

'Can it, Lou!'

'You're wasting your time, Mitch,' he went on, undeterred by the veiled threatening element in the other man's tone. 'She's the type who goes for officers, but I doubt if even officers would be fool enough to try, or even want, to take her on. There's something mean about her,' a thoughtful note entered his voice, 'in her, eating at her. She's got problems, and that means trouble, buddy, take my word for it. Get someone nice and uncomplicated like Pam. By the way, you can drop us off at her apartment and take the car back to the barracks. I'll get a cab back in the morning . . .'

Without even being aware of it, Gina had reversed back up the stairs, one step at a time, everything in her baulking in incredulous horror. So this was how men saw her! This was how they spoke about women. Nausea curled in her stomach. She felt sick—sick with anger and disgust. She had to get out of there . . . but just as she was about to turn, Pam came tripping down the stairs behind her.

'Hi. Have you forgotten something?'

'I—I thought I'd left my ring in the ladies',' said Gina, thinking quickly, 'but I've just remembered, I didn't wear it tonight.'

'That's a relief, then,' said Pam, issuing a sigh. 'Because if you had left it up there, I doubt whether it would still be there now. Are the men down yet?'

'Yes—yes, I think so.' And with a sinking feeling, Gina continued down the stairs with Pam to where the men, now silent, stood in the foyer.

Gina carefully avoided all eye contact with Mitch from that moment on, and after they had driven to Pam's flat, where they parted company with her and Lou, a silence existed between them which neither felt disposed to break until Mitch pulled up at the kerb outside her home.

He had barely switched off the ignition before Gina's hand came down on the door handle. 'Thank you,' she said, her tone void of expression, 'for this evening.'

'I'm sorry it wasn't very enjoyable for you.'

Gina shrugged, opened the door and as she climbed out she said: 'Pubs just aren't my scene.'

'Pubs?' He had also emerged from the car over which the street lamp shed its direct light.

'Bars,' she interpreted for him. 'Goodbye, Mitch.'

He had rounded the car and before she had managed to retreat back far enough across the pavement, he had reached out and grasped hold of her hand. 'I'd like to see you again.'

The prospect appalled her. Violently she wrenched her hand free. 'No, thank you!' She turned hastily away and crossed to her gate, which was shaded by an archway heavily laden with clematis. What made her look back at him, she didn't know. It was an involuntary impulse and one which she instantly regretted. She was already sufficiently shaken and upset, and to see him gazing after her, slowly shaking his head, before swiftly rounding his car, slipping in and driving away, served only to rile and unsettle her further. How dared he feel sorry for her! How *dared* he! With trembling fingers she unlocked her front door and entered the silent stillness of her house. The street lights spilled freely through the curtains, illuminating the kitchen and lounge. She locked the door and went through to pull the curtains in the lounge, but then changed her mind and headed for her bedroom instead.

Who was he, to feel sorry for her? Just who did he think he was? With angry jerks, she drew the curtains in her room together and then systematically stripped off all her clothes and dropped each garment into her cane laundry utility. Despite the lateness of the hour, she knew she simply could not have got into bed with her hair reeking of smoke, so she stepped into the shower and washed herself thoroughly from head to foot.

When she had calmed down sufficiently, she would make believe this disastrous evening had never been. She would purge the entire distasteful experience from her mind just as she did the smoke and grime from her hair and body.

However, she lay in bed as taut as an over-wound spring, writhing as, of its own volition, her mind played and replayed in relentless detail the events of the evening. She lay on her back staring wide-eyed and yet blindly up at the ceiling. She was too upset to sleep, she had to finally admit. In her there was a curious desire to cry, but it had been a long time since she had cried— and it would be a long time before she would again, she vowed vehemently. She turned on to her side and dragged the pillow down further under her neck and cheek. Besides, she couldn't even if she had tried, for already her distress was hardening and moulding itself into that indissoluble core already lodged deeply within her. That core formed a bottle into which she had, over the years, forced all manner of pain, sense of betrayal and rejection. Her emotions she had kept on ice, never used and safely encased within that bottle. In five years she had effectively quelled all desire for a man's company even before it had had time to be born, and this evening was nothing if not a confirmation of how right she had been to set herself such a pattern—a path in life to follow.

Why then should she just want to curl up and turn her face and sob into her pillow?

After a fitful sleep, Gina awoke and was aghast to discover that she had slept in until ten-thirty. She hated to waste her life by sleeping away too many of the precious few hours of freedom. There was so much to be done.

However, by the time evening arrived, she found she had completed only a portion of the tasks she had set for herself that day. Daydreaming was a pastime which, as a rule, she never indulged in, but throughout that day she had often come to to find that time had been frittered away when her concentration had strayed from the job in hand. She couldn't even recall the nature of the thoughts or distractions that had engrossed her, and Sunday passed by in much the same way, with her wandering restlessly from one occupation to another when usually she would have experienced no difficulty whatsoever in becoming totally and happily absorbed in anything she settled to do. Finally, after having taken her gardening tools out from the shed, and stood looking at them for the best part of five minutes, she resolutely stashed them away again, gathered up her swimsuit and towel and key to the car and made off in her car in the direction of the beach.

CHAPTER THREE

GINA watched the deft movements of the hairdresser as he cut at least three inches from her hair and even more from the strands he combed forward over her forehead. Eventually he brought into being two wings of ash-blonde hair flicking out from either side of a fringe that was shaped to part slightly in the middle. As he began the blow-drying process, and the end result began slowly to emerge, Gina finally accepted that she was in good hands and relaxed. A sense of expectation gripped her and quite by accident she met her gaze in the mirror and saw the expectation registered in her expression. How different she looked! And the difference owed nothing to her new hairstyle.

'She has a sexy mouth.' The words jumped unbidden into her mind. Mitch's words. As on several other occasions thoughout the week, she found herself in a position whereby she had to try immediately to reject them, thrust them far from her mind. She wanted to banish them from her memory for ever, along with every other aspect of that unfortunate evening. But she didn't succeed, for in this instance the mouth she was looking at wasn't as controlled or its line firmly compressed as usual, instead the lips were parted and naturally relaxed, revealing the clean straight cut of her lower lip and the straight downward angle of the two sides of her upper lip. She was surprised. She hadn't seen her lips looking quite so full for many years. When had Mitch seen her in such a moment of repose? Her gaze slipped up over her other features, her straight nose with its exquisitely formed nostrils and tip, to her eyes, quite unremarkable in shape and size, but lined thickly with short dark lashes which emphasised their brilliance and dark grey-green colour. Her newly cut hair, being curved under by the hairdressers brush, reached to the base of her long slender neck. The style and length both flattered and softened her squarish bone structure and gave her a new and overall feminine look. Gina bit at her lower lip and for the first time began to doubt the wisdom of her decision to get her hair cut.

She made the appointment on the spur of the moment as a desperate last measure to lift herself up out of the mists of vague depression which had persisted to overshadow her since the weekend before. As she sat examining her new softer image, she could only hope the gambit would pay dividends.

It didn't.

The actions she employed in the carrying out of her work were automatic, but her spare time, of which there had usually never been enough, had been injected with a restless, rather disquieting quality. Another week slipped by, at the end of which she had entered a stage where she had begun to dread the prospect of going home.

The house no longer felt like a haven and while in it she could settle to nothing. She could no longer see any point in finishing the sanding down and redecorating of the kitchen. After fifteen minutes, she would give up, overcome by an enormous sense of futility, and take to wandering aimlessly about the house, searching her mind for a clue as to what to set herself that would wholly and satisfactorily occupy her. She tried all the avenues she knew and usually enjoyed—reading, listening to music, gardening, craft work, painting—but their length was covered quickly and at the end of each one the same blank wall rose up to greet her.

Sleep eluded her, and at this her frustration was compounded. Yet another evening had been spent in idleness, and as if that wasn't bad enough in itself, she had to spend a great deal of the night in wakefulness, rueing the waste.

In the hope of at least overcoming one problem, she decided to take to walking the streets of the quiet neighbourhood before bedtime, breathing in her fill of the fragrant cooler air of the summer nights. The end of her first such venture found her in tears, and in the darkness and loneliness of her attractive home, she changed into her nightgown and lay on her bed weeping disconsolately into her pillow while her heart yearned and cried out a name that had occasionally over the years taken her unawares and slipped out past her lips. How a man such as J.P. Mitchell had the power to open up and exhume an area of her life which she had been congratulating herself on having successfully eradicated from her mind and heart and buried for ever and force memories of the heartache she had experienced to once again flood her being, she simply couldn't understand.

Gradually, towards the end of January, there came signs that her disposition was beginning to return to what she considered was normal. It was such a relief to her, for there had been moments when she wondered whether or not she was on the verge of an emotional collapse. Now this possibility struck her as being quite ludicrous. How could she have ever thought it? she wondered as she put her hair up into a French pleat, tied a narrowly folded scarf about her forehead and drew on a light coral-coloured linen jacket over a matching T-shirt and baggy cream trousers. She set off on what she hoped would be the last of her long evening walks. Not that she hadn't gradually come to enjoy them, but she was now way behind in her schedule and time to enjoy such luxuries wouldn't be so plentiful

So taken up with her thoughts, she walked as far as Main Street, which wasn't the course she would have taken had she become conscious earlier of where her steps were leading her. However, she continued on, turned right into Main Street and began to walk up towards the hotels and the numerous restaurants, fish-and-chip shops and take-away bars which fronted the street.

She didn't dwell too much on the prospect of passing them. It was around hotel closing time, admittedly, but it was so wonderful to feel as though she was again entering that peace she had strived so hard and so long to establish that she felt uplifted enough to confront anything.

How wrong she was she very swiftly discovered. She stopped dead in her tracks and was distantly but positively aware of her colour receding.

They had emerged from one of the hotels and were standing on the pavement with only a matter of yards separating them from her. Lou was with Pam and Mitch was with a girl who appeared both attractive and well groomed and whose stance was relaxed yet graceful. Her features were no more or no less attractive than were Gina's, but there was something present in her expression that she knew full well wasn't and never would be in her own. Something that lit up and animated her countenance and put a sparkle of vivacity in her eyes. There was warmth in her laughter, promise in the shape of her mouth and a love of life evident in every relaxed line of her.

With an effort, Gina dragged her eyes away from her and immediately they clashed with Mitch's. Her heart stood still and the last traces of colour fled from her face. Her reaction was spontaneous. At all costs she had to avoid the foursome, and in order to do so she turned and stepped off the pavement. It was an action that was prompted by panic and void of all thought or plan. Dimly she heard the sound of a horn blast, of squealing tyres, and was momentarily dazzled by the onslaught of bright lights, but the only thing that bore any real significance for her was the slamming into her of the object which seemed to be hurtling towards her and the pain that followed.

She lay quite still, too stunned and later too frightened to move. The first face she saw belonged to J. P. Mitchell. Grim and pale, that which she had wanted to avoid loomed over her. Desperately she tried to get up, but felt a restraining weight on her shoulders.

No! She didn't want his hands on her. Couldn't he see she hated it? She didn't want him near her! She struggled to be free and once free to rise so that she could show them she was perfectly all right, but the pain in her side suddenly made itself felt and with a distressed cry she was forced to fall back on to the pitted bitumen surface.

'Lie still,' Mitch commanded her, a curious blend of harshness and gentleness in his voice. He was taking off his jacket to spread it over her. 'Lou's gone to phone for an ambulance.'

'I don't want an ambulance!' she exclaimed, grasping his coat and throwing it aside. 'Just help me up!'

'You're not to move.' He rested his palm against the top of her head and she pushed agitatedly at his hand until he removed it.

'All right then, I'll get myself up!' Gingerly, though with a determined outward show of unconcern, she rose into a sitting position and ignoring her pain slowly dragged herself to her feet. How curious—the surface of her skin felt so cold and wet. Had it started to rain? She looked around and the anxious face of Mitch's female friend swam before her vision. She allowed herself a smile of grim satisfaction before giving a soft exclamation of wonderment as the world about her tilted and swung in wide, ever-expanding circles.

Mitch caught her and lowered her once more to the ground. She stared up into his face and into those of all the other people who were now milling around, and suddenly she was very frightened. Her fear must have communicated itself to Mitch, for he touched her pale clammy cheek with the back of his fingers. 'There's nothing to worry about, Gina. There's no serious damage. You're going to be fine. You're in shock, that's all.'

She turned her face away from his touch and obligingly he withdrew his hand. Someone had placed a car rug over her and through the throbbing of her pain she heard the sound of a siren drawing closer and closer. She was lifted on to a stretcher and then up into the ambulance, only seconds now from being shut away from all those eyes staring at her as though she was some alien being who had just descended among them. But what she coveted above all was to escape from Mitch's ever-watchful, ever-fathomless gaze.

The doors swung closed and turned her head, a low moan escaping her before she could clench her teeth against it. Soon, mercifully, they would give her something to deaden the pain. She opened her eyes and gave a start as she saw that the only person in the ambulance cab with her was Mitch. 'What—what are you doing here?' she demanded querulously.

'You might need someone.'

'I don't need anyone,' her tone strengthed, became almost belligerent, 'and I certainly don't need you! So please go away.'

He gave a half grin. 'To oblige you might be a little difficult just at the moment. If I tried, I might end up in hospital right alongside you, and I'm sure you wouldn't relish that prospect.'

Her mouth tightened and her lips compressed.

'Someone should contact your parents—perhaps I could do that.'

'I'll decide whether or not my parents should be contacted. Don't you dare interfere!'

'What about a close friend, then?'

'Mind your own damn business!' Treating him to her icy militant stare for a second or two longer, she deliberately averted her head and never looked at him again from that moment until he left the hospital.

Days passed and for the most part Gina slept, oblivious to her surroundings and the time passing. On the third day her sense of awareness returned in ever-increasing degrees. At one point she opened her eyes to find herself starring straight at Mitch, who was sitting on a seat near the edge of her bed, his eyes trained intently upon her face. Why did he always have to watch her like that? As though he could see inside her head and feel pity for her because of what he was discovering there. With a whimper of distress she twisted her head on the pillow, wanting to turn away from him, only to find that her body, stiff and sore and as heavy as lead, refused to obey her.

The next time she saw him the view she was given was of his back, a powerful well-muscled back tapering down to slimmer hips, outlined against the window out of which he was staring.

'Why don't you go away!' she cried, but her voice emerged slurred and husky. He turned, but she couldn't remember whether he answered her or not.

But that he had no intention of heeding her repeated mumbled requests to 'leave her alone', was quite apparent, for he seemed to be seated by her bed or somewhere in the room each time she awoke.

'Haven't you got anything better to do?' she enquired of him as she awoke one afternoon to find him seated by her bed, his elbows resting on his knees while his chin, in turn, was propped up by the platform formed by the meeting of his knuckles. His eyes, brooding and reflective, were as direct as usual and fixed on her pale face.

He straightened, giving her a half smile that seemed to Gina to be faintly whimsical. 'No, quite frankly, I haven't. I like looking at your face in repose. It's a very interesting face.' His hand moved, of its own volition it seemed, and the back of his fingers came up as if to administer a gentle caress to the side of her face.

Gina jerked her head away, but quick though she was, she was not successful in avoiding altogether the contact he made with her. Her mouth hardened and her eyes flashed. 'Well, you may like watching people while they sleep, but I don't like being watched. And I don't like being touched all the time.'

He made a slightly rueful grimace. 'Do I touch you all the time? I apologise. You appear so forlorn sometimes, lost and vulnerable, I guess I kind of like to extend a little comfort if I can.'

Gina spluttered, momentarily at a loss, then: 'I can assure you that I'm none of those things. And what I'd like you to do is to stop bothering me. Just go away and don't come back!' She thumped a clenched fist down on the white cotton counterpane as she spoke and glared at him.

'Why are you so hostile?' he asked, throwing up his hands and bringing them down with a slap on to his knees. 'Is it that I personally pose a threat, or do you have a thing against all men in general?'

'Oh, yes,' Gina gave a mirthless laugh. 'I was wondering when that one was going to come out. Invariably when a woman repudiates a man then the man's way of salving his vanity is to accuse her of finding him a threat or "having a thing" against all men in general. How typical! Why don't you just get it into your head the way it is? I don't like you—that's the plain and simple fact of the matter.'

'Why don't you?' he asked, rubbing the underside of his chin across the tips of his steepled fingers. His heavy brows were raised in a quizzical fashion, deepening still further the grooves carved across his brow.

Gina allowed her eyes to slip distastefully over his face, over the deep slashes on either side of a wide firm mouth and the lines beneath and beside his blue eyes, shallower than the other creases in his face but just as noticeable. He had a straight but aggressive nose, just as aggressive and pugilistic as the strong wide squarish thrust of his jaw. The column of his neck was exposed and appeared as strong and unyielding as the rest of him. His hair, short and straight, was dark, almost black, and while it looked clean and shiny, to Gina it resembled what she suspected his nature to be, wild and unruly. Health and vitality and masculinity, all these ingredients and more exuded from every pore of him, repelling her. Her shudder was ill-concealed as she told him: 'I don't like anything about you.' She spoke without hesitation, unworried about hurting his feelings, convinced that any sensitive points he might have would have to be as bulkily padded and as blunt as he was. 'You're too obvious. I particularly don't like precipitative, persistent, physical men—who have an over-supply of teeth,' she added for good measure, and waited for his response, uncaring of what form it took. However, whatever she might have unconsciously expected, it wasn't that he should throw back his head and laugh with delight and abandonment. She stared at him in amazement. He had an attractive laugh, infectious but far too gusty—and he *did* have too many teeth.

'I think you and I need to come to some understanding,' he said, sobering, although his eyes still sparkled: probably like the sunlit waters of Waikiki, Gina thought, her lips curling in derision. 'You have some pretty unfortunate traits yourself. For example, a sense of humour that's gone missing, a perpetual morose hangdog expression and a disposition and repartee that I can only assume comes from taking vinegar on a fork for breakfast every morning, but for all that, I still like you.'

Gina lay quite still, continuing to meet his mildly challenging gaze for some time after he had spoken. Then suddenly as she felt her eyes darken and as her vision blurred, she turned her head aside. She clenched her jaw and swallowed back the weak inexplicable tears welling in her throat. 'It's of no consequence to me what your opinion of me is, or whether you like me or detest me,' she told him, speaking distinctly. 'Now I'd like to sleep, if you don't mind. When you go this time, please don't come back.'

He rose. 'Okay—you sleep. I'll go, but I'll be back. I think you're in need of a friend—in spite of yourself.'

Gina's head whipped around. 'I have friends!' she exclaimed, her temper now thoroughly aroused.

'Two, according to the hospital staff I've spoken to. Only two other visitors besides myself, and they were a married couple.'

Gina gasped, almost overcome with rage and a sense of helplessness as he confidently and knowledgeably exposed further areas of her own vulnerability. 'How *dare* you poke and pry into my private life! I'll have you know that when I find I need more friends than I have already, *I* will choose them. Right now I'm totally happy with the ones I have—and they don't include *you*!'

'If you were "totally happy", honey, you'd have been up and out of this hospital days ago.' He went on, battering her relentlessly with clubs of truth: 'The car that hit you was merely pulling in to park, not a contender in the Grand Prix. Your injuries were minor, and yet because of your mental and emotional state, it's taken you this long, five days, to emerge from the shock you suffered.' He stopped abruptly. 'Perhaps I've overstepped myself, but I think you needed to be made aware and perhaps to question the lifestyle you've adopted for yourself. No man's an island, you know

No woman either.' Gina felt the dry hardness of his palm as it settled briefly on her head, then she was alone, left to face the inevitable unpalatable prospect of her mind slipping inexorably back over all that had been said.

True to his promise, Mitch came back to visit her again the following two evenings and on both occasions she tolerated his company, responding laconically to his questions and listening apathetically to the content of conversation which he intended to be cheering by peppering it generously with amusing anecdotes of life in the Army.

On the eighth morning, Gina was discharged. To a certain extent she was still stiff and sore, but this incapacity was the least of her worries. What truly daunted her was the thought of returning to her lovely but empty house and the life Mitch had described, devoid of friends and companionship. A life that she had made for herself and with which she had been thoroughly content until Mitch appeared on the scene, determined to strip away and destroy the fragile substance of her self-woven cocoon.

Why had she let him?—but she hadn't, she quickly justified herself. To have stopped him would have taken a personality as preponderate as his own. And she just wasn't so equipped and was further disadvantaged by her impaired health. Did she have what it took to begin to build up again the kind of life she had convinced herself she had wanted? Or didn't she want it any more? As she packed the clothes her friend Mandy had fetched for her, she felt perspiration gather under her arms and down her back and her heart began to beat far too quickly and erratically. If all that she had was taken away and her plan and ambitions for her life destroyed, what would she be left with? What was there anywhere to replace all that would be subtracted? Precisely nothing.

And because fear and uncertainty had crept into her life, into her mind and heart, she decided against resting at home for several days before returning to work. Instead she went back immediately, thus allowing herself less time to dwell on the disruptive forces presently active in her life.

The following Saturday was the second in February. It dawned bright and clear with the sun blazing down from the bright blue expanse that was its home. As the morning wore on the heat intensified. The moisture was sucked from the air until all living things appeared to be gasping. Flowers drooped, the ground hardened still further and trees wilted, while the ranges shimmered, becoming less distinct as a heat haze enveloped them. Other areas of the country were experiencing similar weather conditions, with the threatened drought a fact and bush fires breaking out indiscriminately in the more susceptible areas. On television, the South Island's Canterbury Plains resembled a desert and in the North, the forests were veritable tinderboxes in which all work had been suspended and the fire risk gauges had been set at 'extreme'.

Gina began the day by applying herself to the task of sanding down the walls in the kitchen. Despite the fact that she worked at a leisurely pace, mid-morning found her bathed in sweat. This factor, plus the dull ache that had started up down her injured side, forced her to give up and decide to take a cool shower.

She had barely emerged from the shower when she heard a series of heavy thuds on the glass panes which rattled the back doors. Who on earth could that be? she wondered, leaving on her head the towel that had served to protect her hair from the powerful jet of water and reaching for another. This she wound about herself and padded quietly out into the passage, waiting apprehensively to see if the knocks would come again. They did, but were accompanied this time by the sound of a door opening. Her heart froze and both hands came up to clutch at the join at the top of her towel.

'Hi there. Anyone home?'

Mitch! Her fear turned swiftly to incredulity. The nerve of that man had to defy all description!

'Gina!'

She darted into her bedroom as she realised that if he

had the gall to enter uninvited into the kitchen then it was more than likely he would take it into his head to go on a tour of the house.

Bristling with indignation, she hurriedly pulled on to her still wet body the clothes she had laid out on the bed, calling out: 'I've just got out of the shower!' and could only hope that he didn't consider it the normal thing to do to come into her bedroom to chat to her as she dressed. Clothed finally, she went out to the kitchen, hot and flustered, dragging her fingers through the fringe of her uncombed hair as she went.

'Well, good morning,' he greeted her, rising from where he had seated himself near the table, and this gesture irritated her. Despite the liberties he took, his manners were something she couldn't fault him on, and since she regarded him as unrefined and oafish she found it difficult to align these traits with the others.

As if he was powerless to check himself, his eyes dropped to the length of bare leg her cream shorts revealed and up over her thin strappy green T-shirt which clung, emphasising both the line of her full bust and the fact she had failed to dry herself properly. His expression registered surprise, albeit agreeable surprise.

Gina felt herself flushing under his stare and was suddenly angry with herself for having clothed herself so hastily without giving sufficient thought to the nature of her dress in the light of the change in her circumstances. She glared at him and stepped behind one of the kitchen chairs, gripping its woodcarved back.

'Do you usually sleep in so late?' Mitch asked, glancing at his watch, in no way abashed.

'I was up at seven—if it's any business of yours!' she snapped. 'Do you always barge into people's houses uninvited?'

'Not usually, no.' He quirked an eyebrow at her. 'But I knew if it was left to you to invite me in, I'd spend the duration of my visit on the doorstep. It's a nice place you have here,' he added, looking about him, grimacing and nodding in appreciation.

'I'm so glad you approve,' she said sarcastically, and at that moment heard a gurgling sound coming from the direction of the bench. She turned puzzledly and saw a plume of steam rising from the spout of the electric kettle. 'I didn't turn that on,' she frowned.

'No—I did. I thought you might welcome a cup of coffee before we go to the baseball match.'

Gina's jaw dropped and she gazed at him flabbergasted. 'Just what right do you, a perfect stranger, have to come into my home and take over as if you own the place?'

He pulled a face. 'A perfect stranger? Still? How long do people have to know each other in this country before they consider one another friends?'

'Friendship is a two-way street, haven't you learned, and you're walking it all alone. How many more times do I have to tell you? I don't happen to want a friendship with you.'

'Well, I guess it's just like you said. I'm a pretty forceful kind of character and I don't like taking no for an answer. So how about that coffee?'

Gina crossed over, jerked out the plug from the power point in the wall, and turned to face him, folding her arms and leaning one curved hip against the side of the bench. 'I don't drink coffee, I don't like baseball, I don't like fast friendships—in fact, I don't think there's much at all I do like about the American way of life. So I suggest that you just toddle off back to where you came from—or better still, why not stop wasting your time with me and go gatecrash your attractive, dark-haired lady friend? I'm sure she'd appreciate your attentions a lot better than I do.'

Mitch grinned at her, and there was something about the gleam in his eye that made her distinctly uneasy. He didn't move, yet there was an energy emanating from him that made her want to take a step or two backwards. With a considerable effort, she managed to hold his stare and stand her ground.

'First of all, you're right, Jennie's an attractive woman, warm and generous, but I happen to prefer blondes with cold green eyes. Second, I don't think there's much about life, American-style or otherwise, that you do like or even know how to enjoy. And last of all, I intend to give you a few lessons. Now, go and change into something that won't distract the men from the game at stake and we'll just about make the first innings.'

Gina remained exactly where she was, thin-lipped and narrow-eyed, her pose indolent and her arms still folded.

A smile tugged at the corners of his wide lips. 'Do you really think you're ready for such a drastic first lesson?' he asked lazily. One eyebrow had risen very slightly as he spoke and the challenge that was missing from his tone was there in that one barely perceptible movement.

Gina had straightened and was free-standing almost before she realised it. What would he do? Just how far would he go? When it came right down to it she knew she wouldn't put anything past him. Gritting her teeth and seething inwardly, she marched towards the door that led out into the passage. Before reaching it, she turned and thrust a finger at the double french doors. 'From now on those doors will always be locked!'

'A very minor strategem,' he said, and laughed infectiously. She attempted to snuff out the laughter in his eyes with the ice of her own, but eventually conceding failure, she swung away in the direction of her room.

How was she going to rid her life of this infuriating, interfering clod? In place of her discarded shorts and top, she donned a loose boat-necked T-shirt horizontally striped in colours of navy, brick-red and olive green and a matching olive green skirt, softly gathered and with large pockets. Slipping her feet into heeled sandals and gathering up her purse, sunglasses and hat, she was ready and still nowhere nearer to hitting upon a solution to her problem.

She sat beside Mitch in his rented car, maintaining complete silence throughout the drive. 'We'll see how long it takes before he wearies of this,' she thought to herself, staring resolutely out of her side window.

Upon their arrival at Colquhoun Park, he locked the car and came around to her side, and before she had time to realise his intention, he had taken her hand in his. Her recoil was instantaneous and because he had been fully expecting such a reaction from her, his fingers were quick to tighten about hers. 'Let me go!' she fumed, trying without success to jerk and wriggle her hand free. 'Just because you've succeeded in bullying me to accompany you here, it doesn't mean to say I'll tolerate being mauled by you!'

'Lesson number one,' he told her, starting off across the vast sports field pulling her after him. 'And if you'd just relax, you might learn to enjoy it.'

They reached an area where thirty or more men, outfitted in coloured and numbered bibs over white baseball uniforms, were spread over and beyond the diamond shape that was the baseball pitch. Male voices shouting unintelligible orders, the occasional smack as the leather met leather and the louder crack of the bat making contact with the ball followed by cheering from the small band of spectators, were all sounds which drifted to Gina's ears which were already humming with the extent of her fury.

'Hi, Mitch!' came a shout. 'Over here!'

Dismay churned through her, souring her disposition still further. 'A regular David and Jonathan, aren't we?' she murmured sweetly.

'Not for long,' Mitch replied easily. 'Lou doesn't like you either.'

'I'm heartbroken,' she replied, and drew her breath in sharply as he pulled her hand against him and sandwiched it firmly between his own and the hard length of his thigh.

'Oh, it's you!' was Lou's involuntary, or was it voluntary, exclamation as he saw the face of Mitch's companion, which was concealed to a certain extent by the brim of her straw hat.

Gina bestowed upon him a cold disdainful smile. 'Disappointment all round, I can assure you. Never mind, I'm sure that between us we'll be able to convince Mitch here, that like East and West, never the twain shall meet.'

Lou ignored her and switched his attention back to

Mitch. 'Pam and I are sitting on the grass over there.'
He indicated with a wave of his hand. 'Join us if you
want.' Without waiting for an answer, he turned and
stalked off.

'Well, I'm glad to see that someone else disapproves
of our association,' said Gina, 'even if it is for different
reasons.'

'Which means that I've got you to myself and you've
got me to yourself.'

'I must have been born lucky,' she murmured. 'Do
you think I could have my hand back now? There's
nothing worse than prolonged contact with hot, sweaty
flesh.'

Mitch turned unhurriedly to look at her and the way
his heavy-lidded gaze slid over her features, and his very
expression, caused a tide of fierce heat to well up and
flood every corner of her, rising even to stain her neck
and cheeks, but although she could effectively block his
penetrating searching stare by turning her head, there
was no escaping the low timbre of his voice as he said
slowly and quite seriously: 'On the contrary, such
contact can be very pleasurable indeed. Did he never
show you?'

Her head whipped around. 'Who?' had been about to
spring to her lips when the sound of a heavy leather-
covered ball whined through air quite close to them.

'Hey, Top!' a player yelled. 'Get that for us!'

As Mitch jogged off after the ball, Gina knew
intuitively that she had been given a reprieve and just
how important it was that she avail herself of it. She
turned and, on legs suddenly unsteady, made for a spot
located not far from the bulk of the spectator crowd.
Her vision was blurred and her throat was working to
swallow the lump that had become painfully lodged
there. On sitting down on the withered prickly grass,
she searched in her handbag for sunglasses that would,
in this instance, be donned to serve a dual purpose.
Linking her arms about her drawn-up knees, she gazed
without seeing at the players and remained so
positioned even when Mitch came to rejoin her.

She knew that it was her and not the game he

watched as he lounged back on one elbow beside her. She could feel his eyes on her, taking in every detail of her still, rigidly averted profile, the tilted set line of her jaw, her neck, arms, waist and hips, and ankles just visible. She was as sure of his eyes on her as she was about the content of his unspoken thoughts, and her body shrieked in protest from the discipline she exerted over it to keep it from moving even a muscle.

'You smell nice,' he told her suddenly.

She didn't stir other than to nudge her sunglasses farther up on her nose. 'Most people do when they've just stepped out of a shower,' she said casually, deliberately smothering a yawn with her hand.

'Tired?' he asked.

'No. Bored.'

'Mmm. I guess baseball, like any game, can be boring if you don't understand it. I'll explain it to you as they play.'

Gina raised her eyes briefly to heaven in supplication, as if calling for replenishment of her precariously depleted strength and tolerance. He had to have the thickest hide she had ever encountered in anyone, of that she was positively convinced! Then abruptly and without warning her sense of irritation was usurped and replaced by a desire she hadn't experienced for a long time and one that had become almost foreign to her over the years. But she simply couldn't fall back on the grass crying with laughter. Mitch would really consider he had won a stronghold in her life then, and there'd be no getting rid of him. But the mirth bubbling up within her seemed to come from a source over which she had no control, rendering her peculiarly weak and helpless. She lowered her face to her knees, able to keep silent her laughter but incapable of stilling the shaking of her body.

'Gina?' She felt his large warm hand on her shoulder and curiously experienced no urge to repudiate him. She lifted her head, took off her sunglasses, wiped the tears of mirth from her eyes and looked around at him.

'Very well,' she capitulated. 'Tell me about the game. Are they all Americans?'

'No, not all. Just one or two over from Schofield playing in the Army team. The other team is a local one, I understand.' And patiently he explained to her the rules of the game, but after a further two innings, it came not as a surprise to her that she should reach the conclusion that baseball was not a game to interest her.

'I'm still bored!' she declared, and with another yawn, she lay back on the grass and dropped her hat over her face.

'Then I've got an idea!' And before she could remove her hat to look at him, Mitch had taken her wrist and was pulling her without preamble to her feet. Taken totally by surprise, she was too busy snatching up her belongings to utter any form of protest.

Forced to run to keep up with him, and to prevent her arm being pulled from its socket, she conserved her energy by keeping silent until they had reached his car.

'Wh-what was all that about?' she panted.

'We'll go back to your place and you can show me around. You have an interesting place—I like it. And then, while you fix us lunch, you can tell me all about yourself.'

Gina gaped at him. Then, recovering swiftly, she pulled her arm free of the grip that had loosened and become gentle, and although his hand had in fact been still, she couldn't shake off the impression that it had actually been caressing her wrist. 'You have the most colossal cheek I've ever come up against!' she exclaimed.

Mitch grinned impenitently. 'Then I'm glad. If you'd had a dose of just what the doctor ordered before my coming to New Zealand, we might never have met.' And he left her to ponder on that remark and extract the meaning behind it while he unlocked the car.

With a sigh, Gina climbed in and fastened her seatbelt.

'Have you given in?' he enquired before starting the car.

She swung her head around to look at him. 'About lunch, do you mean?'

He made a face and turned the key in the ignition. 'That'll do for a start, I guess.'

Gina said no more but sat back and remained silent beside him as he drove competently on the left hand side of the road, requiring no directions from her.

How strange she was feeling! As though all at once disorientated, wanting every now and then to giggle, but she knew that if she did she wouldn't be able to stop. The animosity she harboured for the man at her side seemed to have drained away, at least for the moment, and in its place was a kind of peace that bore no similarity to that which she had been fighting to regain ever since he had entered her life. It was as if her laughter at the sports ground had blown the cork from that bottle present somewhere within her, releasing the pressure it was being forced to contain and leaving her feeling as though she had imbibed freely of champagne. She would have to be careful, she told herself, massaging the side of one temple with the tips of her fingers. And get a hold on herself, for if she didn't she could break down in front of this man and it wouldn't be laughter but tears that would win out.

A very subdued Gina took Mitch on a tour of the house, thankful that she could adopt for herself a façade—that of hostess.

'So this is your home? It belongs to you?' Mitch asked as he came into the kitchen where Gina was preparing a salad.

'To me—and the Bank,' she replied, tearing lettuce leaves and dropping them into a wooden bowl.

'How long have you been living here?'

'About three years.'

Mitch came to lounge back against the edge of the bench at which she was working. 'You were very young to get a loan from the Bank.'

'My parents helped me by putting up half the deposit. I've been very fortunate all round.'

'I'd say so, but is this the usual thing for young women of marriageable age here? To buy their own home?'

Gina shrugged, grinding pepper into the dressing and keeping her eyes on her task. 'I don't think so. As a rule those women with hopes of marrying set themselves up in a flat.'

'So why didn't you?'

She glanced at him briefly before pouring the French dressing over the salad. 'Because I've no desire to marry. I enjoy my work too much.'

'Couldn't you combine the two?'

'No. I've no wish to have to give up the two-thirds of the time I devote to my career to a husband and family. Lunch is ready,' she gestured towards the dining-room. 'Let's go through and eat'.

'What is your career?' Mitch asked as he sat down and helped himself from the dish of ham Gina was offering him.

'I'm in charge of the artists' room at the store where we first met.'

'Oh, yes,' Mitch nodded slowly, 'I remember it. So you're an artist.'

'Yes.'

'Doing display work?'

'Yes. Plus signwriting and window dressing.'

'Were you responsible for the décor in this house?'

'Yes. I did the major part of it.'

'By yourself?'

'Mostly.'

'I admire your taste,' he told her.

'Thank you.'

'There's a lot of hand work gone into some of these furnishings, isn't there? The cushions and these seat covers, for instance. And the macramé light shades and those things holding the plants.'

'Yes.'

'Your work?'

'It's all my work. Whenever the urge grips me, I water-paint, and sketch in charcoal as well. One or two of the pictures you can see are examples.'

'Well, well, well!' As in everything else, he was effusive and frank in his praise also and his eyes were warm with both wonder and admiration. 'You're a bundle of talent, there's no doubt about that.'

In any other circumstances and about anything or

anyone else, Gina would have squirmed at his unconstrained enthusiasm and heartfelt appreciation, but since it was so unaccustomed for her to receive encouragement and praise from anyone, she was quite incapable of monitoring her response to it. Aware suddenly that she was glowing with pleasure and that her mouth had fallen open as she gazed at him with shining eyes, she quickly pulled herself together and lowered her gaze and attention to her meal.

'I can see now how your spare time is very valuable to you. What else do you do that you haven't told me about?'

As matter-of-factly as she could, she told him how she dabbled in the designing of clothes and tie-dying which had to be carried out at work and how even there conditions were not entirely conducive. 'One day I'd like to extend the shed at the bottom of the garden and install all the necessary equipment and design clothes and fashion fabrics full time. But of course that's a pipe-dream and probably not very practical. A hobby might cease to be a hobby if one had to depend on it for a living. Nevertheless, I'd still like to have a go at it one of these days.'

She talked on, needing only one encouraging word to prompt her, but managed to restrain herself from boring him with her entire repertoire of sketches and photographs of the fashions she had designed. Time skipped by and only occasionally did she become aware of blue eyes watching her every movement, the flash of her legs as she went to fetch more coffee, the swirl of the hem of her skirt as she returned, the gestures of her hands whose help she enlisted to embroider what she was saying, and the variety of expressions that ran across the normally immobile terrain of her face.

At his request, she led him outside and showed him the garden shed which she had dreams of enlarging or replacing. This inspection led on to another of the garden. Mitch displayed a deep and genuine interest in the vegetables that she had planted and that were flourishing thanks to the watering she gave them every evening.

'Amazing,' he kept murmuring as he crouched beside the rows to examine more closely the silverbeet, tomatoes and lettuces. Later, he came to join her as she stood pulling beans from their run, and as he reached out from behind her to pick one that she had missed, the underside of his arm brushed over the top of hers, and without thinking, she shrank away from him and moved swiftly to one side. In a state of confusion, she looked up at him and then away. 'I think these will be enough,' she said, her voice cold and stilted to her own ears. She turned to make her way back between the rows of vegetables when he spoke, quietly, asking her a question which caused her to halt abruptly in her tracks.

'Who was he?'

'Who?' The word sprang from her lips before she could prevent it. She looked back at him in what she hoped was a casual manner.

'The man who caused you to become a virtual recluse, withdrawn and introverted, presenting a front to the world that isn't the real you, could never be the real you.'

Gina forced herself to relax, toss her head and laugh naturally. 'You're imagining things! There's no man, and there never has been nor ever will be. I haven't the time. You came across the real me four weeks ago. Sorry to disappoint you, but I've never been any different.'

'I'm not disappointed at all,' Mitch assured her, his blue eyes narrowing, his stare penetrating. 'I saw a glimpse of the real you this afternoon. I'm not going to let you close up on me again.'

Gina drew herself up straight and her eyes became hard and cool. 'You take far too much upon yourself, and even more for granted. Don't presume you know me and what makes me tick. You don't, nor are you likely to, because I don't intend to give you the opportunity!' She turned on her heel and strode over the remainder of the garden and across the small square of back lawn and through the double quarter-paned doors into her house.

'Are you saying you won't see me again?' Mitch demanded as he came up behind her.

'I'm saying exactly that.'

'Why not?'

'That's a rather irrelevant question, isn't it? We have nothing in common.'

'I thought we got on very well this afternoon.'

'I get on with anyone who wishes to discuss my work.'

'And I like the girl who gets so animated when she's discussing her work, so let's summon her back.'

'Don't be ridiculous!'

'I'm sure if she were thoroughly kissed, she would be persuaded to come back,' Mitch drawled, watching lazily as the colour fled from her face.

Gina retreated several steps. 'Don't—don't you dare lay a hand on me!'

'No. Victory that way wouldn't prove at all satisfactory.' And after a short, tense silence, he gave a soft, almost regretful sigh. 'Time for me to go, I guess.' He straightened from his position of lounging back against the bench and smiled at her. 'Thanks for a delicious lunch and a most enlightening afternoon.' And he sighed again, this time with positive regret as he saw her lips compress together. 'I'm only in New Zealand for another six weeks or so, so you can console yourself with the thought that you haven't got long to put up with me.'

'I don't want to see you again, Mitch. I mean it!' and she despaired at the entreaty that threaded the last three words.

'I wrote down your number,' he said, patting his back pocket, 'so I'll ring you before I arrive the next time,' he promised, and with an impudent sideways grin and a casual wave, he passed through the open door and disappeared along the narrow path which took him through the clematis-laden arch and over the small picket gate.

He had gone. Gina crumpled and fell like a limp wrung-out rag on to the nearest kitchen chair. That man! He was insufferable! The ego of him—the arrogance!

However, her relief at his departure and the indignation he had aroused in her began to dissipate almost immediately in the silence he left behind. While he had been there he had seemed to fill the house with his presence, imparting his life and vitality and as it flowed out from him it had seemed to spread, warming every corner of the house. It was this quality in the atmosphere that had gone also, having departed with him, leaving her curiously bereft, restless in the sudden echoing silence. She felt as though the walls were suddenly pressing in on her and she too wanted to get out of the house, escape to somewhere where there were wide open spaces. But, determinedly, she suppressed this peculiar upsurge of panic and instead switched on the radio and began to busy herself by washing the lunchtime dishes and making as much noise as she could in the process.

CHAPTER FOUR

THREE days and nights passed and her phone gave not a solitary tinkle. Tired though she was at the end of each evening, Gina found it difficult to sleep. She refused to entertain the idea that disappointment was keeping her awake. She had been suffering sleepless nights ever since her first encounter with that detestable man, so what could possibly be the cause? Was it linked with him at all, or was there a hidden and more profound reason behind her bouts of insomnia?

On the fourth night, at about nine, her phone rang. She was sitting with her feet up on the couch, reading, when the strident sounds split her peace and sent her heart into a state of siege. Immediately she became uncurled, braced, all the while telling herself that she would be a fool to answer it. But then, reasoned another section of her common sense, Mitch would feel that she saw him as a threat and so become even more emboldened than he was already—if that were at all possible.

Without spending further time speculating, she rose, crossed to the phone and snatched up the receiver. 'Hello,' she greeted tersely.

'Gina? Is that you?'

The tension in her melted instantly and she fell with a sigh on to the arm of an armchair. 'Mum! How wonderful to hear your voice. How are you?'

'Never been better. What about you? Your recent letters haven't sounded as perky as usual.'

'Oh, I'm fine. Actually, I had an accident recently, so I was pretty low for a while, but I'm fine now.'

'What kind of accident? At work?'

'No.' Gina hesitated, then admitted wryly: 'I had an argument with a car.'

'Gina!' Her mother was aghast. 'Why didn't you contact us?'

'It wasn't serious, Mum. There was no point in worrying you needlessly.' And at her mother's insistence, she outlined to her what had happened, glossing over the facts to a certain extent and omitting altogether the true reason her doctor gave for her tardy recovery, that it was more emotional than physical in nature. 'But I'm back to my usual self now, Mum, so don't worry. I'll be home to see you on Dad's birthday. That's only two weeks away, isn't it?'

'Yes, that's why I'm ringing, to remind you.'

Gina laughed. 'I don't need reminding! I'm looking forward to it. I really want to try to get home more often.'

'You know we're planning a party, Gina, and I'd just like you to feel free to bring a friend home with you. Are you going out with anyone?'

Gina chuckled. 'You're ever hopeful, aren't you, Mum?' she teased lightly, 'but the answer's still the same as it was last time. No, there's no one. I haven't time to be involved in more than I am already. How many people are coming?'

'About seventy, roughly. Wiremu and his brothers are organising a *hangi*, so there's no problem as regards the cooking of the meat and potatoes. The rest of the preparations will be smooth sailing in comparison.'

'Would you like me to come home a day or so earlier and lend a hand?' asked Gina.

'N-no, I don't think so, dear. Actually it seems as though I'll be getting some help from a rather unexpected quarter.' Her mother paused and Gina waited for some time before prompting her to continue:

'Yes? From whom?'

'Well, I received a call from Sydney last night . . .'

Those few words were all that was needed to cause her heart to quail, send fingers of ice on a play over the surface of her skin, brushing against the small fine hairs until they stood up on end. She rose slowly to her feet. 'Colette?'

'Yes. She said she thinks she might like to return to New Zealand to live, but she considers the only way she'll be able to decide is by coming back. She thought she'd make the trip across in time for Howard's birthday.'

How carefully and diplomatically her mother had avoided all mention of that matter in connection with her sister that had and always would affect her so deeply. She had obviously decided to leave the initiative of introducing the subject to Gina. And of course she knew she couldn't hang up without learning the answer to the most crucial question. 'And Norrie?'

Her mother's sigh was restrained. 'Yes, and Norrie. I'm sorry, Gina.'

'It's all right, Mum,' Gina responded belatedly, trying to instil reassurance into her voice. 'There was nothing you could do. It's just one of those things.'

'You will still come, won't you?'

'Of course,' Gina agreed, not allowing herself to hesitate.

'Good—I'm glad. Try to bring a friend with you, Gina.'

'I'll see what I can do.'

'Promise?'

Gina managed a laugh. 'I promise.'

After she had hung up, she went slowly through to the kitchen to make herself a drink of Milo made with hot milk. She was going to need all the help she could get to sleep peacefully that night. However, she looked down at the thick pale liquid swirling around in her mug and felt that if she were to drink it she would be sick.

Colette and Norrie. She placed the mug on the unstained wood of the kitchen table, sat down and rested her forehead on the cradle formed by her interlocked fingers. So they were still together. Still living together and still unmarried after all this time. If they were married she was sure her mother would have linked their names right from the outset. How was she going to manage it, to *bear* to meet both of them again after so long? Five years had passed since her eighteen-year-old sister had run off with her fiancé. But even ten years would never make it a day she could forget, because it was one that was burned into the very walls of her memory. On that day she was to have been married.

For the small community in and around Kaimoana it was to have been the wedding of the year. Norrie Freeman, the eligible son of one of the most prosperous farmers in the province, was to wed the popular daughter of a more modest farmer in the same area. It was to have been an event that would have stayed alive for years in the minds of all those in the district. And so it had. But for a reason far removed from the original one.

A radiant bride, dressed in a glorious white creation which she had drafted and made herself and accompanied by bridesmaids also attired in gowns she had designed, had almost reached the quaint old country church when the limousine in which they had been travelling had been hailed by a cousin of Norrie's who had found himself assigned the unenviable task of informing the bridal party that the groom had absconded to Australia with the bride's sister.

The betrayal she had had to contend with on top of everything else was almost more than she had been able to bear. She had known that her sister had been carrying a torch for Norrie. Colette had never attempted to conceal the fact, flirting openly with Norrie whenever the opportunity presented itself, allowing her jealousy of her older sister to drive a wedge between them. She had flatly refused to be her chief bridesmaid and had, instead, become as petulant and as difficult as she had known how.

The reason this had not perturbed Gina too greatly at the time was because she had never seen her sister as anything more than a child who would eventually get over her teenage crush. That underestimation had been her most critical mistake. Colette, she had realised later, had at eighteen not only not been a child but had possibly never been a child. And what had astounded her and opened her eyes to this revelation more than anything else was the realisation that Norrie had been totally bewitched by her sister's sultry baby-faced beauty, her long curling blonde hair and small curvaceous five-feet-two-inch frame, and had desired this package to such an extent he had been prepared to dismiss any feelings he had had for her, his fiancée, to terminate and obliterate them as though they had never existed and write off his reputation, his good standing in the area, his favour with his father and his future on the three-thousand-acre property that had always been his home and inheritance which he shared with his two brothers.

It had been then, at twenty-two, that Gina had learned that there was a quality some women possessed, a kind of charisma, an animal magnetism that drew men both against and in accordance with their wills. This was the essence of the difference between her and her sister. Colette possessed this charisma. She didn't.

She hadn't forgiven her sister for what she had done; for the years of pain and misery she had caused her, but she knew, as she had always known, that this was a bridge she would have to come to sooner or later and there would be no skirting it, for existing between one side and the other was a dark yawning crevasse. Perhaps this was the time to start the crossing. Or was it? She would only know for sure when she saw the two of them again together. But one fact was irrefutable, and that was that she couldn't brave the reunion alone. She would need support. But whose?

Only one name leapt spontaneously to her mind, and she rejected it instantly To invite Mitch to accompny her to Tiraumea was out of the question. She would merely be courting more problems to handle than she had already.

However, as the date drew closer and because the friends she had cultivated were by no means vast in number, she came to accept that she had no alternative.

But perhaps she had thrown away her opportunity to ask him, because he had rung her once and invited her to dine with him and she had turned him down, making her Keep Fit classes her excuse. The excuse was legitimate enough, but her Keep Fit programme with the Y.M.C.A. could be arranged for any hour to suit her. It was more than likely that Mitch was aware of this. However, he was nothing if not persistent, and when he rang again, Gina was given cause for the first time to be glad of this trait in him and she accepted his invitation to dine.

'Why?' was his swift and only response when, during their second course, she asked him as casually as she could if he would like to join her when she travelled to Tiraumea to be with her father on his birthday.

'What do you mean, "why?"?' she questioned, meeting his narrowed, suddenly shrewd gaze.

'I mean, why are you asking me? There must be a reason.'

'Must there?' Gina widened her eyes purposely. 'I suppose I thought you might be interested in going to a *hangi*. The food cooked underground is really quite delicious.'

'That was a very poor try,' he shook his head at her.

'*Hangis* are no novelty once you've lived a while in Hawaii.'

'Oh, of course,' Gina conceded, genuinely having overlooked this point. 'The Polynesian culture doesn't vary that much from island to island, does it? Oh, well, I hadn't ruled out the possibility that you might like to see a little of the rest of the country.'

'Uh-uh.' Again he shook his head. 'I can't see that as holding much water, either.'

'Very well, let's forget the idea,' and she dunked a ring of deep-fried squid into one of the seafood dressings supplied.

'No, I don't think so,' he said. 'I'd like to go.'

But Gina neither liked nor trusted the slow deliberate manner in which he spoke. Fear prickled through her, keeping her eyes lowered as she ate and turning every morsel to chaff in her mouth. She'd never be sure of her ground while she was with this perceptive and unconventional man. Why hadn't she had the sense to remain true to the stance she had originally taken with him?

'I will go with you. And I'll look forward to discovering for myself the reason for your sudden and unaccustomed display of hospitality.'

Assailed then by a sense of despair, she couldn't help looking up at him with eyes flashing, nor suppress the need to give expression to the resentment she felt. 'Yes, you do that!' she snapped with bitterness. 'You're quite clever in your own way, aren't you? Not to mention manipulative, conniving and insensitive. Oh, yes, you'll soon find out what you want to know. If it's not made blatantly obvious, you'll no doubt find vast numbers only too eager to fill you in on the deails.' She dropped her fork on to her plate with a clatter, crumpled her serviette, then pushed back her chair and stood up. 'I'd like to go home now. But I'll go alone. There's no need for you not to finish your meal.' And she turned and made her way out of the restaurant.

She turned blindly into the street, only to feel Mitch's light touch at her elbow reminding her that she should be going in the opposite direction. In silence, he drove her back to her house and pulled up at the kerb beside the picket gate.

With her hand already pressing down on the doorhandle, she half turned to him in the semi-darkness and flashed him a brief glance. 'I'm sorry about tonight,' she said stiltedly. 'And please forget about this weekend. I'll go alone.'

He touched her shoulder lightly with the tips of his fingers, freezing her movements.

'You're not short of manipulative qualities yourself, you know, Gina,' he said quietly. 'No man likes to realise he's being used, even an unrefined insensitive lout like me . . . Oh, I've been well aware of how you view me, so don't go all stiff and defensive on me. If you needed some kind of support this weekend, why couldn't you just come right out and say so?'

'I don't want anything from you!' she disputed.

'No, I know you don't want anything from me—but you certainly need something from someone and I'm the only person around capable of meeting that need. I'll be glad to help you, Gina. Only be honest with me and don't try to use me.'

Anger was so fierce in her now, she was almost choking with it. 'Why, you—you——' she floundered, then clenched her teeth and began again. 'Yes, you are a lout, a clod, a boor and a great deal worse besides. I can't stand the sight of you! I can't bear you to be near me. You couldn't come even close to meeting any need I might have. Do you understand? None. Not even one!'

Out of all the reactions she might have expected to receive from him it wasn't one of mirth. And yet he was very definitely chuckling, that low warm throaty laughter of his that came in response to her diatribe. Then suddenly her body went totally rigid and her indignation was forgotten as all her senses rushed to become focused on the feeling of the hand that had come to rest on the nape of her neck beneath her hair. 'I can assure you, honey,' he said softly, his warm strong fingers moving on her neck, 'that I'm more than man enough to meet everyone of them.'

Swamped with sensations of disgust and outrage, Gina wrenched herself free and within seconds she was standing on the pavement, staring into the car's dim interior, maddened even further by his grin and the resultant gleam of his teeth. 'You're coarse, vulgar and utterly despicable! If you dare to venture on to my property again, I'll call the police, do you hear? And I mean it!' So saying, she slammed the door shut, battling down her urge to follow up the too-soft thud with a kick from her foot.

Immediately the car purred into life and pulled away from the kerb and Gina, with arms held rigid at her side and nails biting into her palms, remained staring after it until its tail lights had rounded one of the corners beyond.

On Friday afternoon, she arrived home early from work and began the task of packing, one which she had been putting off all week. How she was dreading the ordeal stretching before her! Her insides hadn't been functioning normally since her row with Mitch and she doubted that they would have any opportunity to right themselves during the days that lay ahead.

Once the packing was finished and she had showered and changed into a dark rose pink sun-frock, which would make the chore of driving the long distance in the presiding heat a little more comfortable, she brought her small suitcase and other accessories through to the kitchen where she snatched a glass of milk and a quick bite to eat before locking up the house and making her way out to where she had left her car parked in front of the garage. Closing the gate after her, she turned and halted abruptly in mid-stride. Leaning with his back against the car and a beige rucksack at his feet was Mitch. He straightened and came forward to relieve her of her suitcase, smiling as usual.

'What are you doing here?' she demanded.

'Waiting for you. I'd have waited inside the car, but, like the sensible organised person that you are, you locked it. We'll have to travel in yours,' he went on with a slight grimace. 'Lou wasn't too much in favour of being without ours for three days in a row.'

'I thought I'd made it clear I didn't want to set eyes on you again!'

'Oh, come on now, don't start being tiresome—it's too damn hot. You need to at least appear this weekend as though you've got a lover and I wouldn't mind having a look at the kind of farming set-up you have over here, since I spent my boyhood on one back in the States.'

As she had taken immediate umbrage at his reference to her need of a 'lover', her mouth had opened to put him straight in no uncertain terms. Now she snapped it shut and decided her best policy was to ignore him. She went forward to open the boot of her car, casting a glance of disfavour at his gaily patterned Hawaiian shirt. Who of those who knew her would be fooled into believing this man, confident, over-assertive and full of his own importance, could ever possibly be her lover? Certainly not her sister. She almost laughed aloud, a laugh that had it escaped would have been tinged with hysteria.

'Would you like me to drive?' he asked, tossing his rucksack in alongside her suitcase before she had a chance to close the lid of the boot.

She sighed. 'No.'

'Good. I could do with forty winks.'

'Look,' she slammed the boot shut, 'the only place I'm taking you is back to camp!'

Mitch didn't move, but all at once Gina felt menaced by the very presence of him, by the direct unwavering nature of his stare. She sidled away from him in what she could only hope was an unobtrusive manner.

'I'm coming with you, Gina. Whether we establish that fact here or back at the camp is entirely up to you.' Calmly he reached out and took the keys from her suddenly lifeless fingers. He unlocked both doors, the passenger side first, and then held open for her the door of the driver's side.

Tight-lipped, Gina came forward and slipped in behind the wheel. He closed the door for her and came around, slid in beside her and handed to her the keys. She took them from him, suppressing the urge to snatch them, and silently started the car.

'You can't envisage me in the role of your lover, can you?' Mitch remarked once the city had been left behind and they were surrounded by the gold of parched sun-dried fields. He had been watching her the whole while, his eyes on her profile, her neck and on the hands that manipulated the steering wheel, and to pretend to be unaware of his surveillance was exacting a strenuous toll.

Now the nature of his latest asservation caused her hands to jerk slightly on the wheel and she gave a humourless laugh to try to cover up the start he gave her. 'Can you envisage me being yours?'

'I could—if I imposed a little strain on the imagination.'

For some reason Gina couldn't readily define his answer failed to please her and she was annoyed with herself. 'Well, we're certainly not going to fool anyone, you and I. Anyone who knows me will know immediately that for me someone like you would be the proverbial "last man on earth".'

'I can prove them—and you—wrong, of course.'

At this, she darted him a glance. He appeared to be deriving a great deal of enjoyment and satisfaction from the situation—as usual—and the audacious twinkle in his blue eyes made her hackles rise. She knew he wouldn't tell her how unless she asked, just as she knew she would regret it if she did ask. But the question sprang, full of scorn, from her lips before she could stop it. 'And how would you propose to do that?'

For a moment or two she thought he wasn't going to answer her, for he was sliding back his seat and sorting out a comfortable position for himself in which to sleep. 'I could seduce you,' he said, settling himself and resting his head back.

'You mean you could try,' Gina snapped back, her hands itching to strike out at his complacement face and indolently positioned body. 'And perhaps I wish you would. I'd love to be given the opportunity to puncture that oversized ego of yours!'

But aside from a short but full-bodied chuckle, there was no further response to her rather rash challenge, and a brief sideways glance at him revealed to her that he was no longer conscious of her or anything else. He really was the most self-opinionated, infuriating person she had ever had the misfortune to meet!

She drove for a full two hours with only the hum of the car's engine breaking the silence. The road before her stretched on through forever varying countryside, the landscape appearing even more dry and brassy in colour as each mile took them further into the Hawkes Bay province. Earlier on she had draped her short white jacket, edged with dusky pink piping, over her right arm and shoulder to shield it from the fierce rays of the sun which had begun to bite into her skin. And now, because the sun was lowering to meet with the horizon, she found opportunities to remove her sunglasses were becoming fewer and fewer.

With less than forty minutes to go, Gina began to tire. She tried stretching and shifting the position of her limbs which had become cramped from being forced to maintain one position for several hours. By chance she happened to glance at the man beside her and stiffened instantly at discovering a pair of wide-awake blue eyes staring straight at her.

'How long have you been lounging there like that watching me?' she demanded all the muscles in her face tensing. 'I thought I told you that I hated being watched, and especially in that surreptitious way you're always watching me.'

He flashed her a lazy unrepentant smile. 'You've got a delicious mouth. I like looking at it—it has an interesting shape. But,' he sighed, somewhat regretfully, and sat up in his seat, 'when you're aware that I'm looking at you, like now, you kind of iron it out.'

'Until it resembles a compressed paper clip?'

The thrust of satisfaction she felt at sensing him give a minute start of surprise quickly faded as he laughed softly. 'So you overheard old Lou, did you?'

'And you,' she reminded him curtly.

'Pull over here and I'll drive the rest of the way; you look worn out.'

She offered no opposition, but was relieved to do as he bade and be given the opportunity to walk about a little and stretch her legs before climbing into the passenger's side.

'I hope you didn't take what Lou said too much to heart,' said Mitch, and when it became evident that Gina didn't consider this comment worth a reply, he went on: 'Lou's not one to appreciate a challenge. He likes his women as uncomplicated and as easy to read as a street map . . .'

'Turn left up here—Kakahi Road,' Gina cut in deliberately, and although he was smiling, this she could sense, he refrained from speaking again for the remainder of the journey.

The homestead on Tiraumea was large, rambling and one-storeyed, a genuine old Colonial home with peaked gables over jutting double-hung windows, lead-lights on either side of the entrances and a wide verandah which encircled a good half of the house. Although Gina and Colette had been the only children, Gina couldn't remember a time when the house's two spare bedrooms weren't being used. Guests had always been welcome at Tiraumea. Whether they happened to be family, friends, school friends, relatives or children requiring a temporary foster-home, the doors to Tiraumea had always stood open. And judging by her mother's letters, her parents hadn't changed at all in this respect. Even though both daughters were now living away from home, the house was seldom empty.

As Mitch drove up the long sweeping curve that led through tree-studded pastures to the homestead, Gina could hear the familiar sound of dogs barking, hailing their approach and serving to inform her parents that she had arrived.

'It's a charming house,' Mitch said slowly, bringing the car to a halt and switching off the ignition.

Gina remained silent, wanting only to weep as she always did when she saw her beloved home, for the sight of it reminded her that had fate not dealt her such a harsh blow, she would still be living in this beautiful district, under sunny skies amid the hills and near the beaches and in a position to bring her children to visit their grandparents every other day. Instead . . . Instead she was making only a periodic and painful visit home alone—or, her eyes flickered disparagingly over Mitch's violent shirt, as in this case, in the company of this social reject. Without a word, she climbed out of the car and went forward to greet her mother, who was coming down the steps, tall and apron-clad and with fading blonde hair caught softly back from a face wreathed in the smiles of a fulfilled and gracious woman.

'It's good to see you, Mum. You're looking blooming as usual.'

Despite her smile and words of welcome, Phoebe Wells made a careful and slightly anxious assessment of her daughter before enfolding her in a warm embrace. A few seconds later, she straightened and her arms slowly fell from about her. 'Well, well,' she exclaimed, 'I see you've changed your mind after all, Gina. I'm so glad!'

For a second or two, Gina was left wondering what her mother meant, until she turned to follow the direction of her gaze and saw Mitch approaching them. 'Oh, you mean him? Yes, well, I suppose you could say I changed my mind.'

'Or else you could say I changed it for her, Mrs Wells.'

As cocksure as ever and exuding what he probably considered to be charm, Mitch came forward with a hand outstretched. 'I'm J. P. Mitchell, ma'am. Just call me Mitch.' And he wrung her mother's hand with frank pleasure and exuberance.

Covertly, Gina watched to see the reaction this forceful, vibrant personality would have upon her mother. At first the older woman appeared quite nonplussed, but she rallied quickly and smiled at the man with a corresponding pleasure that was so obviously genuine that Gina almost fell back in stunned amazement.

'I'm pleased to meet you, Mitch. Where do you come from, and how long have you known Gina?'

'I'm in New Zealand as a member of a visiting

Company from Schofield Army Barracks in Hawaii, and I guess you could say that Gina and I have been friends for a couple of months now. Isn't that right, Gina?'

Gina ignored him and explained to her mother: 'Mitch was there when I had that accident I told you about, Mum. He was—very kind to me while I was in hospital. I thought he might appreciate the opportunity of seeing a bit of the countryside, so that's why I invited him up this weekend.'

'I was brought up on a farm myself, Mrs Wells,' he smiled his wide smile at the older woman. 'So in one way and another, Gina and I have a lot in common.'

Gina cast him a portentous look.

'Why, that's wonderful!' Phoebe applauded. 'My husband will certainly enjoy having a chat with you— not only about American farming methods, but also about Army life. He served in the Islands during the Second World War. He'll be glad of someone like you to talk with, won't he, Gina?'

'Yes,' Gina responded with enthusiasm. 'Help me with the luggage, will you, Mitch.' And as Mitch obliged, she spoke to him in low vehement tones: 'I'm warning you now not to go any further with this despicable farce!'

Mitch sighed. Opening the boot, he bent forward, resting his palms along the lower ridge of the boot, and turned his head to squint up at her. 'What are you insinuating now?'

'You know perfectly well what I mean. Don't you dare grease up to my parents and try to ingratiate yourself with them! You're a fake and a phoney, Mitch, while they're terrific genuine people, and I don't want to see them falling for every line that you take it into your head to throw out. I hope I've made myself quite clear!' And so saying, she turned on her heel and strode back to where her mother was waiting at the foot of the steps. With an arm about each other, they went into the house and Mitch followed, carrying their luggage.

'Is Colette home yet, Mum?' Gina enquired rather

reluctantly as they entered the house's richly panelled vestibule.

'Yes, she and Norrie are in the lounge with your father having a drink. We were waiting for you before we started dinner.' Her mother gave her waist a squeeze. 'Don't worry, dear, you've got plenty of support. And I'd say that there'd be as much of that in your nice big American as there is in both your father and me put together. Our loyalties, understandably, have to be divided, but his . . . Well, I'm just so glad you brought him.'

'He's only a friend, Mum. And not even a close one. We don't even get on together very well. We do nothing but fight.'

'It's sounding better and better!' And she gave her daughter another brief squeeze before releasing her, saying in a voice loud enough to be heard by them both: 'I'll leave the two of you to freshen up and join us when you're ready. Mitch, your room is along the passage here next to Gina's, and Gina will show you where the bathroom is.' She touched Mitch's arm lightly, then left them both alone.

Mitch lowered the rucksack to the floor immediately inside the door of his room, and ignoring the purpose for which Gina's hand was outstretched, he grasped the extended wrist and with a jerk pulled her around until she was forced to follow in the same direction as he. Once inside her room, he dropped her suitcase on to the floor and kicked the bedroom door shut.

'What *are* you doing?' Gina gasped, struggling vainly to free her wrist. 'Will you please let me go this minute and get out of my room!'

But she might never have spoken, for far from complying, he pulled her forward and then swung her back on to the bed in a single fluid movement. Stupefied with shock, she lay where he had so roughly and so effortlessly flung her, incapable of thought, word or action. She looked up into his face, and the bleakness there, the steely look of determination in his eyes, struck trepidation right through her. She made to move then, to sit and leap up off the bed and out of his reach, but his reflexes were a thousand times swifter than hers. Catching both her hands, he pushed her back, thrusting her arms up over her head while the weight of his body came down across her own. She managed to bite back her cry of distress but could do nothing to muffle the dry rasping sounds of the breathing of one in the grip of panic.

For some indeterminable time, as he remained looking down silently into the face of his prey, she expected to see mirrored in his eyes a certain peculiar pleasure she was sure he was deriving from mastering her and rendering her so utterly helpless, but there was none. Instead she saw open contempt written there—for her.

Incensed at being forced to receive and tolerate that which she didn't consider she had earned but that he had, she strove to be rid of the weight of him, but succeeded only in causing him to bear down more heavily upon her until she knew that every hard powerful outline of his body was etched indelibly into her flesh.

'Oh, yes, you're a first-class bitch, all right.' He spoke with deceptive mildness. 'There's no two ways about that. I've let you get away with a great deal, though it's obvious you've been so preoccupied with yourself, you've failed to realise it. But one thing I won't tolerate from anyone and that's being called a phoney. There's only one phoney around here, my frustrated little shrew, and that's you. There's not one honest thought floating around in that snooty upper-class little mind of yours nor one honest bone in any part of your delectable body!'

Pale and livid, Gina glared up at him, hatred for him glittering in her eyes. 'Get off me!' she got out through clenched teeth and barely moving lips.

'When first you tell me what it is is about me that you find so repugnant.'

Gina's laughter emerged as a shrill high-pitched sound. 'We can hardly remain like this all night, can we—and that's how long it would take!'

'Just one thing will do.'

'Well, how about your shirt, then?' she threw at him. 'The colours are bilious!'

Mitch didn't hesitate. Rolling a little to one side, he grasped handsful of the back of his shirt, drew it over head and tossed the article across the room.

Suddenly Gina seemed to experience a new difficulty with her breathing. Their eyes met and she felt as though he was thrusting her beneath the surface of some strange, dark, bottomless lake, submerging her, robbing her of and absorbing into himself her strength, her will and her very life. He watched her, his face and eyes still steady and quite inscrutable, as her hands, now free, tried to push him away, only to find that her palms couldn't maintain that required continued contact with the hard wall of his chest. Their distracted, ineffectual fluttering eventually ceased and her fingers curled until two clenched fists lay on the bed, one on either side of her head. Her face, stiff with distaste, turned aside from the sight of him.

'Quite a fastidious wench, aren't you?' Mitch observed mockingly. 'I should really give you something to be fastidious about.' And as he spoke he slowly, gently raised his body a fraction, moving it as if in a caress over hers, at the same time drawing a leg up between her own in such an intimate way that a gasp had escaped her before she had been given time to think to recall it. Desperately she tried to press back and away from him, shrinking and stretching in an endeavour to escape his purpose. But her efforts were futile, as her struggles succeeded only in exposing to the fullest extent her neck and shoulders. She held herself rigid and still and heard herself whimper like a stricken animal as his breath, moist and warm, fanned her neck, followed by the rasp of his shaven skin ... Then abruptly his head and half of his body lifted.

'Whoops! . . . I *am* sorry!' The sound of Colette's voice penetrated her battered senses. The astonishment in her voice turned to amusement, that derisive derogatory kind that Gina remembered so well. 'I came to see what was keeping you. Something far more enthralling than the prospect of dinner, obviously. Shall we start without you?'

'We'll be right along,' said Mitch quite calmly, lifting himself up off the bed and drawing Gina with him. And Gina looked on mutely as her sister treated Mitch to a slow deliberate appraisal, her gliding light blue eyes mirroring appreciation as they swept him from head to foot.

'Right, then,' said Colette slowly, her tongue in cheek. And managing to tear her eyes off him for a second, she spared her sister a mildly incredulous glance before turning with a jaunty toss of her long blonde hair, and disappearing through the doorway.

Gina watched as Mitch's eyes lifted from the spot from where Colette's well curved rear, clad in brief white shorts, had disappeared, and swung to meet hers. 'Does your sister usually openly devour all your men friends with her eyes like that?' The inevitable amusement had returned, alight in his eyes and threading his voice.

'I wouldn't know. She's been living in Australia for the past five years,' Gina said tightly, 'but right now this is the the only thing I'm concerned about.' And with eyes blazing, she lifted her hand and struck him fully across the mouth. 'Don't ever manhandle me like you've just done again! Treating me as though I was the type of flotsam and jetsam you're no doubt used to associating with—and under my parents' roof as well. You're contemptible!'

All trace of humour in him fled. His nostrils dilated and his eyes narrowed, glinting ominously. 'And it's because this is your parents' house that I won't retaliate to that. But I'm warning you now, Gina, don't try that one on me again.' He crossed to gather up his shirt from the floor and she quickly stepped out of his path. 'Tap on my door when you're ready for dinner.' And the door shut quietly behind him.

Aware suddenly that she was trembling from head to foot, Gina sank down weakly on to the cane chair, which she herself had bought from a jumble sale some years before and stripped and revarnished. As if she didn't have enough to contend with, without this unpredictable, *undisciplined* savage on her hands as well! She raked the fingers of both hands through her hair and buried her face in her palms. Never had she been subject to such barbarity or acts of blatant crudity as Mitch had just exhibited. Throughout the two-year duration of their courtship, Norrie had always treated her with the utmost respect and gentility—something which a man of Mitch's suspect breeding and background couldn't be expected to understand, much less practise. He was like an animal who responds to its baser instincts. If he had never known anything better in his life how could one expect from him a higher standard of behaviour? Finally satisfied with her own analysis of Mitch's character, Gina forced herself to move. After a quick wash she ran a brush through her tangled hair, straightened the twisted body of her dress and considered that she was as ready as she was ever likely to be to face the trial still before her.

At least two years had passed since she had last tried to envisage what her reaction would be the first time she came face to face with Norrie. After he had jilted her she had always known that they would meet again one day, but she had never suspected that a five-year period would elapse before they eventually did so.

By the time she had reached the lounge she was as taut as an elastic band stretched to its capacity. Dimly she was aware of Mitch taking her arm as they entered the room, and when his touch was not immediately withdrawn she did not repel it but was curiously grateful for the support it was unwittingly, or was it wittingly, extending her? She would never be able to tell with Mitch.

Both her father and Norrie rose from their chairs as they entered the room. Although she was aware of Norrie, tall and fair as she remembered, rising to his feet, she found she couldn't bring herself to look directly at him until after she had introduced Mitch to everyone. This formality out of the way, she greeted her sister, extending her hand to Norrie and quickly went on less formally and less inhibitedly to embrace her father, who wasted no time in suggesting that they begin their dinner and led the way to the dining-room, his arm still about his elder daughter.

The dining-room was a room used only in the evenings; during the day they dined in an area set aside in the comfortably large kitchen. But Gina liked best the occasions such as this when they sat on chairs with velvet-covered seating and at a large oval-shaped mahogany table across the centre of which her mother placed on mats steaming dishes of meat and vegetables and jugs of sauces and hot gravy. The room was her favourite, with its vast Persian rugs, open fireplace, the magnificent walnut dresser and the tall double-hung windows which reached down almost to the floor and opened on to the verandah. The modest chandelier gleaming above them shed its soft radiance, adding richness and warmth to an atmosphere which already owned all the qualities that made a house of solid construction and sound foundation a home which was just as sound and secure.

Her mother's prediction was right, Gina soon discovered. Mitch and her father hit it off immediately, and for the life of her, Gina couldn't understand why. Wasn't she made up of part of this man who was chatting and laughing so easily with the American? In which case, why didn't she find with Mitch at least some of this rapport? She stared at him sourly and noticed that he had donned a clean short-sleeved shirt, this one unpatterned and all one colour. Well, at least that was something, she conceded, and as she looked away, her gaze collided with Colette's which was resting on her alight with mockery and amused interest.

'Where did you manage to come by him?' she asked in a tone that told her she approved in every way of her choice.

Gina's glance darted to Norrie and away again. It was difficult to determine whether or not he was in any way upset by Colette's undisguised admiration for the American. His face was still as closed and as bland as it had been the first time her gaze had skidded across his in the lounge and had seen his eyes, the colour of wild honey, in the process of travelling over her. They had met neis without the slightest qualm. Not even a hint of shame, guilt or remorse at what they had done to her five years before was reflected in the attitude of either Norrie or her sister, and the indolence in his eyes and the carelessness of his manner were two aspects of him she couldn't remember him having possessed before.

'Mitch is just a friend,' she said without thinking. 'Nothing more.'

'Just a friend?' Colette echoed. 'Well, you must have changed pretty drastically, then, over the last few years. If I hadn't seen the clinch you two were in with my own eyes, I'd have sworn that a man like Mitch would have been far too hot a property for you to handle!'

Impaled by shock at her sister's improprietous observations, Gina could only stare at her, turning hot and cold in turns and only vaguely aware of the silence that had fallen on all those at the table.

'If you come into this house, Colette,' said her mother quietly at last, 'then I would require you to bring with you the manners you were taught here. I hope that's understood.' She rose to her feet and began to gather up the empty plates.

'Yes, Mum,' Colette said dutifully, but by no means contrite.

'Who's for dessert?' her mother enquired.

And as Gina continued to stare at her sister, she received a sudden insight into her sister's character, and the revelation left her feeling sick to her stomach. She hadn't been the primary target for her malicious barbed remark, only the secondary. All the time she had spoken, Colette's eyes had been fixed on Norrie, watching to gauge the reaction, if any, her indiscreet disclosure might have on him. Did she receive a reaction, one that she could recognise? Gina wondered, her eyes moving to Norrie's poker face, his eyes downcast as his long shapely fingers arranged his dessert fork this way and that on the pattern woven into the cream, satin-finished tablecloth.

He had changed, she thought, and her heart began to ache. She couldn't remember him ever having been so indifferent, so lethargic. He still looked the same, however, even though the Australian sun had darkened the golden tan of his skin and bleached even lighter the upper layers of his longish silky dark blond hair. Yes, he looked the same Norrie she had been prepared to marry—different from Mitch in every way. Fair, not dark. Boyish, not aggressively masculine. Handsome and athletic and slightly aristocratic, not looking or built like a coarse pugilist. Resentment darkened her eyes as she glanced along at Mitch, only to find him lounging back in his chair with his amused eyes looking back at her. She stiffened and defied him with her withering stare, but it had no effect on him whatsoever. The corners of his wide mouth dropped in a rueful grimace and he shook his head and closed his eyes momentarily, opening them again so that they could ask her silently: 'What *are* we going to do with you?'

Deliberately she rose, took the gravy boat up in her hands and carried it out to the kitchen, and knew from the chuckle that followed her departure that he had guessed full well what it really was she would like to have done with it.

CHAPTER FIVE

GINA rose at eight-thirty the following morning to find that preparations for that evening's *hangi* in her father's honour were already under way. Her father, Phoebe told her, had taken Mitch off on a tour of the four-hundred-acre farm, and Gina merely shrugged in response to this information, being considerably more interested in the whereabouts of Norrie and Colette. Both, she soon learned, had gone out for the day, leaving the burden of the party arrangements on the rest of the family and the goodwill of friends. Of whom there were many, Gina noted gratefully. Food for the *hangi* was the first priority, and Wiremu Ikaka had his project well in hand. By mid-afternoon cold meat, salads and desserts had been prepared. The trestles had been erected in the garden, dressed and set up with the essentials such as serviettes, plates, cutlery, cruets, glassware and other necessary items. Lanterns had been strung up across the lawn, extending to link one tree with another. A makeshift wooden platform had been assembled for those who had volunteered to contribute and combine their musical talents and for the benefit of any guests who might wish to dance. It was a fairly sizeable platform, and as Gina looked with favour upon it, she had no way of knowing the embarrassment she was going to have to suffer because of it.

One by one their helpers had come and one by one they had left, until the only chatter to be heard in the garden was that of the birds.

'Well, I think that's about all we can do for now,' said Phoebe, coming up alongside her daughter. She slipped an arm around her and with her spare hand shielded her eyes from the sun and gazed critically upon the scene before her. 'How do you think it looks?'

'It couldn't look better.'

'Have we forgotten anything?'

'I don't think so. Even if we have it could soon be rectified.'

'Hmm, I suppose so. No sign of your father or Mitch yet?'

'No. What on earth can they be finding to do all this time?'

Phoebe shrugged. 'Your guess is as good as mine. Knowing your father, I wouldn't be a bit surprised if he hasn't sneaked Mitch off to meet the locals at the pub.'

'And knowing Mitch, I don't think he would require much persuasion,' Gina rejoined dryly.

'He's quite a man.'

Gina looked at her mother curiously. 'Do you really think so—or are you just saying that?'

'No, I'm not just saying it. I mean it.'

Gina shrugged, finding it easier to simply accept her mother's opinion and not try to understand what it was she and Colette apparently found so admirable about him.

'But you don't, it seems?'

'He's not my type.'

Phoebe inclined her head in neither agreement nor dis-agreement. 'I must admit he's not in the least like Norrie.' And at this, she felt her daughter's back stiffen under her arm. 'Are you still carrying a torch for him, Gina? Even now, having seen him again, after all this time?'

'I—don't know,' Gina owned up slowly. 'He's changed.'

'He has,' Phoebe nodded. 'And he would have anyway, if he'd married you. I don't say that he would have changed the same way, but I think he's the type of person who changes according to his circumstances and allows himself to be shaped and moulded by the situation he's in and the people about him. I think you'd have been too strong for him, Gina, and your expectations of yourself are high. I think he knew, though only subconsciously, that he would never have been able to measure up to your strength and expectations.'

Gina looked away abruptly, swallowing convulsively and blinking back a sudden onrush of tears.

'Colette, I think, is a capricious creature, quite without conscience or scruples. I'm sorry for her and I often weep for her when I try to imagine what will become of her.'

'You don't think they'll stay together?' Tear-bright eyes turned on her mother in astonishment.

Phoebe sighed. 'I don't honestly know. In a way I hope they do, because in a way they seem to suit each other. A strange pair. Colette's my own daughter and I love her, but I feel I've never known her.' She smiled at Gina and turned, keeping her arm outstretched for Gina to turn within it. 'Let's go back to the house. I could do with a cool shower, a drink and a good rest before the inundation!'

After taking a shower, Gina lay on her bed in a lemon cotton housecoat and pondered on what her mother had said until she eventually dozed off, waking again to find the sunlight sloping at such an angle into her room, she knew it must be getting on for six o'clock. She rose, dressed in a sun-frock of a navy silk-like fabric, applied make-up sparingly but with her customary skill, and drew her hair back into a pleat, flicking at the winged sides of her parted fringe with a comb.

As she walked into the lounge, three pairs of eyes turned on her, and she immediately summoned all her defences, caution among them.

'Don't tell me you've been in bed all day?' Mitch greeted her. He had risen to his feet. 'You were there when I left this morning and there when I came back this evening.'

Gina's eyes hardened and cooled as they rested on him. 'Well, the last time I saw you was last night,' she managed sweetly. 'You had a drink in your hand then and you've got a drink in your hand now. I hope that doesn't signify you've been drinking all this time.' Their eyes held and temperaments clashed silently.

'Come and sit down by me,' was his soft reply, after his compelling eyes more than met the challenge in hers, forcing hers to drop first.

Avenging herself, she became even more obdurate and taking delight in ignoring him, sat down gracefully on the arm of the armchair nearest her.

'The way you two speak to each other,' Colette mused from her curled-up position beside Norrie on the couch, her heavy lidded gaze shifting lazily from one to the other, 'it's difficult to believe that you're lovers.'

'Is it? Why?' Mitch was asking before Gina had time to correct her sister's unthinkable assumption. 'I haven't heard the two of you together strike a harmonious note yet.'

'But Norrie and I have been together five years.' Colette turned to Norrie, watching him closely, trailing the tips of her painted nails along his bare arm. 'We understand each other, don't we, darling? Besides, we strike harmonious notes in other areas which more than make up for the wrong ones . . .'

To Gina's surprise, Norrie stood up abruptly and asked her if he could fetch her a drink.

'Er—yes, please. I'll have a shandy.'

'And *I'll* have another Scotch on the rocks,' Colette

ordered, holding up her glass. His face quite impassive, Norrie took it while Colette returned her attention to Mitch. 'Do you and Gina strike harmonious notes in other areas?'

'That's enough, Col!' Norrie spoke without intonation, surprising Gina still further.

Colette pouted, looking up at him through her lashes, and grinned up at him impishly when he handed her her glass. 'I'll tell you later how I found them, and perhaps you could be as masterful with me as Mitch was with Gina . . .'

Nauseated, Gina rose to her feet. 'Excuse me,' she murmured, and left the room, taking her drink outside on to the verandah and settling herself on the front steps, well away from the lounge and its obnoxious occupants. Although the hand holding her glass was quite steady, she was aware of her insides trembling and twitching like leaves that fluttered in the breeze. How was it possible for two sisters to differ from one another in every conceivable way? Would any reasonable form of communication ever be established between them again, or would she always be so serious and over-sensitive while Colette behaved as though she were the only cat and everyone around her, including Norrie, were mice to be played with? Was she *ever* going to grow up? Would the real Colette ever be permitted to emerge through all the facetiousness, the play-acting, the disrespect for others—through the senseless pointlessness of it all?

So deeply engrossed was she in her troubled ponderings, she failed to hear the footsteps on the verandah boards, but became abruptly aware of the trouserclad legs standing alongside her. She looked up even though she knew instinctively who it was. Without speaking, she returned her gaze to the smooth sun-dappled expanse of parched lawn that was spread out before her and shaded by several giant plane trees, an oak and a horse-chestnut.

Mitch sat down on a step, one down from her, a liberty which compelled her to inform him pointedly: 'I came out here to be alone.'

He settled himself more comfortably with his back against the balustrade, crooking one leg and stretching straight the other. 'I thought you might want to know where I've been and what I've been doing all day.'

'Then you thought wrong.'

In response to which he gave a wry laugh. 'Maybe I should have said I *hoped* you might want to know. I already know there's nothing about me that interests you.'

'Except one thing,' she turned on him suddenly, her eyes flashing with accusation. 'Why did you let Colette believe we were lovers?'

Something akin to expectation had flickered momentarily in his blue eyes before dying, to allow a rueful amusement to take its place. He drew up his outstretched leg and looked down through bent knees at the two steps on which his feet, one on either, were resting, and the laughter that followed was short, soft and self-deprecating, as though he was being forced into admitting some sort of defeat. 'Your sister,' he said, looking up, 'wasn't interested in knowing whether we were lovers or not. I doubt if she knows whether or not she even believes we are. I'd even go so far as to say she couldn't give a damn one way or the other. There's a game your sister's playing, but I haven't as yet worked out what it is. Which it humbles me to admit, because I don't believe for a minute that she has what it takes to make a complex character, but I guess that whatever she lacks in substance, she more than makes up for in wiles and cunning.'

'And you being so open and uncomplicated, you consider you're in a position to judge, I presume?' Gina enquired sardonically, an impatient shrug her only response to his silently made request to smoke.

'If you'd just cast aside your preconceptions and prejudices, which we could all acquire if we allowed past experience to shackle us with them, you'd find me as uncomplicated and as easy to read as you are,' he told her, lighting up a cigarette. 'We're alike, you and I, not that you'd have the honesty to admit it. Only I'm not confused. I know what it is I want ... Don't run away!' His hand shot out and grasped her wrist to stay her as she rose to her feet, unable any longer to withstand the intensity of his gaze nor understand the peculiar heat that was rising in her at what he was saying. 'You're always running away, aren't you? From yourself and a destiny of which you aren't the author, of which you aren't in control.' His hand released her wrist and he sat back in an attitude of relaxation as though supremely confident that she would do as he bade her.

'I'm not always running away;' she felt she had to defend herself. 'I've nothing to run away from.'

'You ran when your sister snaffled your man right from under your nose, didn't you? You may have made a physical stopover in Palmerston North, but you made sure that everything else that goes into making up Gina Wells, the very essence of her, kept right on going.'

Gina stared at him icily. 'Where did you find out so much about my private affairs? No matter how ingratiating you've been, I can't believe my father would betray me . . .'

'He never said a word,' Mitch cut in. 'But just because you find it comfortable and convenient to go about with blinkers on, I don't. I don't consider I'm a genius at having arrived at that conclusion. It wouldn't go astray if you learned to be more perspicacious and not allow yourself to be ruled by the superficial nature of your feelings. You're not a superficial person, not like your sister, predominantly shallow with sudden deep dark holes into which unsuspecting men fall. Be positive. Get to know, not what you don't want, for God's sake, but what you do want!'

'Such admirable attributes, and all of which you're in possession of, naturally. How perfect we are!' Her sarcasm, though weak, was her only defence.

In his slumped relaxed position, inhaling on his cigarette, Mitch looked at her, his eyes narrowed and smiling in such a way that Gina felt a resurgence of that peculiar heat, the effect of which made part of her want to bolt for her life and thus stem it, while another part of her, a total stranger to her, wanted to remain still and allow the heat to invade where it willed.

'I've always known what I wanted,' Mitch told her, 'and I know now what I want.' And Gina was ensnared by his gaze, compelled and unable to look away. Then he sighed softly, as though acknowledging that he aspired in vain. 'But then I'm a man, not ruled by sentiment or the past. There's no time for past memories, only the present realities. Don't go on wasting yourself, Gina, throwing yourself away because of what happened in the past, counting it as loss when all the while it was gain. By rights you should be thanking your lucky stars. He wasn't man enough for you then and he's not man enough for you now. Colette did you a service, if you'd but realise it, and reaped the dubious benefit for herself.'

'How can you *say* that?' Gina flared. 'You didn't know him then. He's changed.'

'Good heavens above, girl! I didn't have to know him then—or now. One look has told me all I need to know. When are you going to get your eyes opened? If he'd married you, I'd have felt more sorry for him than for you. He'd never have survived!'

Indignation and a sense of grave injustice welled up and swept over her. 'Thank you very much!'

'And you would be in a worse state now than you are now. You're quite a woman, Gina. If you must waste yourself, waste yourself on a real man, not on the memory of a poor pale imitation.'

This was the ultimate provocation, the one that goaded her to the limit of all she intended to endure. She was on her feet and this time there was no thwarting her. 'Your effrontery is unbelievable!' she got out, struggling for coherence. 'You leave me gasping! Speechless . . .!'

'And spent,' he injected, also rising, but more leisurely. 'Yes, I could do.'

In any other circumstances his implication would have been totally lost on her, but for some reason his allusion couldn't have been starker had it been written on her understanding.

Her breath was indrawn with a hiss. 'If that's what is on your mind,' she said with quiet but unmistakable emphasis, 'then let me tell you here and now, you're wasting your time.'

'Honey, I believe it,' Mitch assured her. 'I'm just trying to ensure that the men you may meet in the future don't waste theirs and that you won't suffer even greater loss.'

Tuned in as she was to this particular wavelength, Gina couldn't fail to catch the significance intended behind this comment. Her lips thinned and her eyes, more grey than green, were like flint. 'Your ego must surely be posing a problem for you. If it becomes any larger I'm certain you'll develop a hernia from having to carry it!'

At this, Mitch broke into spontaneous laughter and his laughter, rich and unimpeded as always, promptly relegated Gina to floundering in a state of helpless fury. Turning on her heel, she strode away and left him.

She had in no way thawed in her attitude towards him when the time came for her to sit down to dinner beside him, with her mother on the other side of him and her father, Colette and Norrie seated on the opposite side of the trestle.

While laughter, chatter, gaiety and music abounded all about them as friends and relatives of the family all rose to the occasion and contributed to Howard's birthday celebrations, Gina felt curiously detached from the festivities, unable to expel her own personal sense of unreality.

'I hope you approve of my choice of shirt this evening,' Mitch said to her as she tackled the succulent aromatic pork and kumara and a variety of salads for which she had no appetite. Recognising at once his intention to bait her, Gina ignored him, forked a little of the meat into her mouth and looked up and straight ahead of her, and as she did so she caught Norrie's rather contemplative stare resting upon her. She smiled at him, a smile as forced as her appetite, for inside her seethed chaos out of which nothing natural could possibly come. With Mitch taunting her on one side and Norrie's brooding ever-watchful stare on her on the other, what hope did she have of enjoying equanimity?

The evening slipped by, with all events working in harmoniously together. Some people ate while others danced. Some sang, others related amusing jokes or anecdotes about Howard and his life and contributions to the community, which, all were adamant, was the richer for having known him.

After speaking at length with Phoebe, Mitch again turned his attention to Gina and speaking in soft undertones, asked her to dance with him.

This time she responded and looking with a deliberately vacuous stare, she gave him her laconic refusal.

He gazed back at her steadily before saying, 'I don't think I'm going to take no for an answer.'

Gina clutched her hands together beneath the flap of the linen table cover and found the courage to meet his stare with intransigence in her own.

'I'll dance with you, Mitch,' came Colette's voice, and as Gina glanced across at her, she realised that this wasn't the first time that evening she had noticed Colette's light blue eyes alighting on Mitch, nor the first time she had seen that almost feline hunger expressed openly in her face. 'I'd love to dance with you.' And she stood up, extended a dainty hand across the table to Mitch and waggled it impatiently.

Gina could feel Mitch's eyes still upon her, but she didn't look at him again. She sensed him look briefly towards Norrie, guessed that Norrie must have given some form of silent assent, because Mitch took Colette's hand and they both moved up on to the erected platform.

A sharp inexplicable pain, like that delivered by a double-edged sword, pierced through her at the sight of the two of them, particularly Mitch's acceptance of her sister's small curvaceous body pressed against his own so snugly that not even a blade of grass could have been slid in between them. She told herself it was disgust, not for Colette, for Colette was like a kitten, intent only on play and its own sensuous pleasures, but for Mitch,

who presumably knew better and yet made no move to
discourage her.

In silence, Norrie stood up and appealed to her with
his eyes, and she found herself responding to their
honeyed magic as she had always done from as far back
as she cared to remember. Trembling started up within
her at the mere anticipation of being in his arms again
after the endless aching for the feel of them for so many
years. Would she melt as she had always done? Would
she succumb to the tide of sensation which had left her
in a state of mindlessness and clinging to him in
shivering, feverish anticipation of the lowering of his
mouth to hers? She had to find out.

Her discovery, made almost instantaneously, left her
stunned, aghast and with an almost overwhelming call
to weep. Had it in reality been like this, and had that
which she remembered existed only in her imagination?
Norrie's frame was tall, thin, with a strength that came
into being in response to the command of his own
desire. The purposelessness, the lack of vitality and life
waned, but only as his body was governed by instinct
and responded in kind to her proximity. His arm
brooked no withdrawal as he drew her close and held
her tightly against him and his breathing sounded
laboured against her ear.

Incredibly, she found herself swallowing back her
revulsion and trying to struggle free. 'Norrie,' she
whispered fiercely. 'Norrie!' Reluctantly, he drew back
a little, grazing moist parted lips across the side of her
temple in the process. He gazed down at her, his heavy-
lidded slightly smiling eyes telling her as frankly as his
body the effect she was having upon him.

She felt sick and unnerved. Did he lack every
vestige of decency and self-control, or did he simply
have no wish to employ any? With her or with anyone
else, for she refused to believe that she herself had
aroused him but that he would have responded in this
execrable self-indulgent manner with any reasonably
attractive woman who, on a whim, he took into his
arms.

'What's the matter?' he enquired softly, not allowing

the lower part of her body to be separated from his. 'You didn't used to object, I remember.'

And at his words the memories she had considered sacred for so long were suddenly stripped of the perfection in which she had been determined to keep them encased and in an instant were sullied, defiled, reduced to ashes. She struggled with her thoughts and emotions, desperately anxious not to reveal to him how distracted she really was.

'No, I didn't, did I? But I've grown up even if you haven't. I no longer appreciate the superficial or living on the surface of life.'

Norrie's smile curved mockingly on his well-shaped, well-defined lips. 'Don't tell me you've plumbed the depths with that rambunctious, rough-edged American?'

'Mitch is first and foremost a man!' Gina retorted, not dwelling on her astonishment at hearing herself leap to his defence, but jerking her body determinedly back from all contact with his. 'And that means he always ensures that he's in control of himself and the situation. I'd like to return to the table now,' she requested stiffly, and offering no further opposition, Norrie escorted her back to her seat.

It was an enormous relief to be able to give in to the pleas of her quaking limbs and to be free of the arms that she once was convinced she couldn't live without and which now she knew she never wanted to feel again. She shuddered and sensed again the urge to weep. She watched expressionlessly as Mitch and Colette, exchanging comments and laughing uproariously, returned hand in hand to the table.

Beside her, Mitch swung one leg over the form and then paused to reach out to cup her chin in his hand and tilt up her face. 'Cheer up,' he urged softly, and dropped swift kiss on the tip of her nose.

Inexplicably tears sprang to her eyes and she lowered her lashes quickly lest he saw them.

'Mitch!' A hand descended on Mitch's shoulder and in response to it Mitch released her and straightened. It was Wiremu Ikaka standing behind him, a wide smile creasing his brown face and mischief twinkling in his eyes. 'How about teaching us Maoris, and *pakehas* too, how they do the hula in Hawaii?'

Mitch's heavy brows lifted in waggish amazement. 'You mean you can't do the hula?' he exclaimed, responding in kind. 'And you call yourselves Polynesians. Aw! I ain't never met a Polynesian yet who couldn't do the hula!'

Laughter came from all around. 'Well, come on, then,' Wiremu challenged him. 'Let's see you put your hips where your mouth is.'

'Okay, you're on. I hope you can play the tom-toms.'

'I've never yet met a Maori who couldn't,' Wiremu riposted.

Mitch laughed and without looking at her, he reached down to grasp Gina's hand and attempted to pull her to her feet.

'Wha—at are you doing?' she gasped, resisting automatically.

He looked at her then, his blue eyes alight with a lively sense of fun. 'You and me, honey, are going to demonstrate the hula.'

'But I can't . . .' she protested.

'You can. No such word as "can't" in Hawaiian!' and as he spoke he grasped her waist and lifted her effortlessly over the form. Then, taking her hand once more, he led her, her feet dragging, up on to the platform.

He released her hand and left her to stand by and watch, squirming inwardly with embarrassment, as he bent to roll up his trouser legs and then tuck up the bottom of his scarlet shirt, this one liberally patterned with darker red palm trees and sunsets, until his midriff was bare. Gina watched this procedure with ever-increasing dismay, wondering what he was going to do next. Then realising suddenly that she was actually free from his grip, she turned to escape back into relative anonymity at her father's table. But she had left it too late. Those hard warm fingers closed again over her wrist and swung her around as the beat of the tom-toms struck up. He lifted her arms up above her head, demonstrated briefly how she was to manoeuvre them and then brought his attention to their hips and the movement required of their legs.

To her astonishment she discovered that he could indeed dance the hula, and remarkably well. But nothing on earth was going to induce her to rotate her hips like that . . .! Then, at that very moment, as if her decision had been inscribed on her forehead for him to read, Mitch took her hips in his hands and much to the delight of the watching guests, tried to coerce them to imitate the undulating movements of his. She baulked, and felt his clasp tighten immediately. Her gaze flew up to encounter his, smouldering with silent laughter and devilry, and she knew by the persuasive pressure of his hands that he intended to induce her hips not only to sway seductively but to advance to meet his. Her arms lowered in a flash and she shoved at his hands with her own. Surprisingly, they put up no resistance and a second later she was free and she fled off the platform and made her way, pale and shaken, back to her seat.

To behave with poise and her usual composure called for every ounce of self-will she possessed, particularly when all the while she was aware of Norrie's expressionless steadfast gaze resting upon her, not to mention her mother's snatched concern-filled glances and her father's occasional solicitous patting of her arm.

It didn't take her long to gather together her scattered wits sufficiently to realise that Colette must have been up to take her place even before she had stepped down from the platform, and for this Gina had to acknowledge she was grateful. Gradually, as her vision cleared, she was able to focus her gaze on the two figures on the platform. To witness Colette's expertise in an area where she had failed held no surprise for her, only pain, a pain which twisted like a blade in her throat. With eyes strangely a-glitter in a colourless poker face, she watched Colette turn her back to Mitch and nestle her swaying, well curved posterior seductively against his hips, before turning her head and lifting her laughing face to his.

The ache in Gina's throat became excruciating, and becoming aware that her hands had met together and clenched themselves, she thrust them down on to her lap and out of sight. They suited each other, the two of them, lost in each other like a couple of pagans, dancing a pagan dance to the arousing beat of pagan drums. Yet she suspected that only she saw the excitement, the brazen invitation in her sister's upturned face, for everyone else present was laughing and clapping their appreciation and many even began to clamber up on the platform to join them.

Colette had 'snaffled,' as Mitch put it, her fiancé right from under her nose, on her wedding day too, but it was not at Colette they looked askance, rather at herself. Colette was the alluring one, the reckless one, the one with great verve and sense of adventure. Nobody ever knew what she would do next, and all waited expectantly. As cute, cuddlesome and playful as a kitten—how could one such as she, so pretty too, ever do any real harm or deliberately set out to hurt anyone—least of all her own sister? No, a trifle irresponsible, one had to admit, but there was no harm in her. In fact the two sisters complemented one another in a way, Gina had heard her aunt say, many years before. One so serious and the other madcap—they balanced each other out.

As soon as she was convinced that no one would observe her slipping away, Gina set out on a long walk, down the drive and out along the verge of the narrow moonlit country road, breathing in the scent of grasses and the wild honeysuckle which sweetened the night air, and listening to the din of the cicadas in the bushes and clinging to the fence posts and power poles.

When some considerable time later she returned, it was to sight Norrie lounging up against the gatepost which supported one of the two halves of the old beautifully fashioned spike-topped wooden gate. A lamp, the size and shape of a child's ball, sat atop the tall gatepost directly above his head and its soft glow alighted on the top of his head and casted shadows over the rest of him.

'Are you waiting for me?' Gina asked a trifle sharply as she came level with him.

He drew once more on his cigarette, then straightened up and pressed out the butt on the post.

'I suppose I must be. I would have walked with you if you'd told me you were going.'

'I wanted to be alone.' Her tone was terse. 'That's why I waited until I was sure you'd stopped watching me like a hawk circling over its prey.'

'I'm not the only one who watches you like a hawk, so you won't lose your American friend to Colette, if that's what you wanted to be alone to agonise over.'

'I'm not in the least bit concerned what Mitch does. Or Colette, for that matter. But I should have thought it would have worried you, seeing Colette making a deliberate play for another man. Doesn't it?' she was goaded to ask when Norrie made no attempt to confirm or deny what she had said.

'So you're still the puritan I asked to marry me!' he laughed, a laugh which she found unpleasant and even vaguely sinister.

She made to bypass him, but he moved with a fleetness of which Gina hadn't dreamed him capable and caught her arm with bony fingers that dug into her flesh. She didn't struggle but remained passively resistant, staring in stony silence into his shadowed face.

'Why,' he taunted her softly, 'I'd even go so far as to wager that no man has taken up where I left off. Not even the macho-Mitch.'

'I thought Colette would have put you right on that score by now,' Gina replied with simulated non-chalance.

'Col's a con-artist, a very clever and adept shyster. I wouldn't trust her if my life depended on it.'

At the enormity of this confession, Gina's mouth fell open and she gaped at him dumbfounded.

'But we're not talking about the inimitable Colette. We're talking about you . . .'

'I don't understand you!' Gina interjected suddenly, her perplexity evident in her voice. 'Why do the two of

you stay together if all you have to offer each other is
contempt and ridicule and mistrust?'

'Oh, we understand each other, all right. We're two
of a kind, I suppose you could say.'

Gina shook her head at him, further confounded.
'You mean to say you walked out, turned your back on
your family and—and spurned the love I had for you
for something so—so sordid, so unworthy?'

'I would have done so anyway, sooner or later.
Darling Gina,' Norrie laughed, 'I see you still don't
understand. In which case you never did love me—the
real me. You never saw or recognised the real me, so
how could you have possibly loved me? But Col did.
And she was the only one who did, because we're
kindred spirits—two of a kind, addicted to one another.
It's like a sickness that neither of us can be free of. But
I've never stopped wanting you, Gina. The perfect
antithesis of Col—Cool, aloof, regal. And I know that
while you may have outgrown your pristine virginal
love for me, I'm willing to stake anything on the
certainty that you still want me as much as I want you.
As lovers we'd be ideal. As husband and wife, we'd
have been a disaster.'

Gina could scarcely believe her ears. Her sense of
outrage had assumed such giant proportions that she
knew words, even if she had had the power to summon
them, would never be sufficiently adequate vessels by
which to give expression to how she felt. Instead she
acted, and the sound of her hand making contact with
Norrie's face was a short sharp crack which was loud
enough to silence all the cicadas in their immediate
vicinity.

'You! Want you!' her voice rang and shook with the
intensity of her scorn. 'Do you honestly think I would
want a treacherous, unprincipled louse like you who
wouldn't know truth, decency or honour if it flew in his
face?' She heard a strangled laugh which she knew to be
but didn't recognise as her own. 'You're out of your
mind!'

Norrie's breath was sucked in sharply and his hands
shot out and fastened themselves around her upper

arms, jolting her forward until she was clamped against him. 'I did you a favour when I ran out on you, you sanctimonious little prig!' he grated. 'The least you can show me is a little gratitude!'

'Gratitude!' Gina exploded, her incredulity and anger increasing, adding vigour to her struggle to drag herself free. 'All I feel for you is contempt. Now let me *go!*'

He laughed grimly. 'Later. When you've stopped struggling and I've felt your magnificent body trembling in my arms—as I did when we were dancing and as I did five years ago on the occasions I'd brought you to the brink of surrender . . .'

Abruptly, she desisted in her strenuous ineffectual efforts to escape as some area somewhere in her brain functioned calmly, telling her what she must do. When every instinct in her was urging her to fight, it was difficult to will herself to relax and become still and pliant in his hands. However, out of sheer desperation, she did so. And as his arms extended to encircle her she brought up her knee, a drastic action she had never before found herself forced to employ.

Norrie swore and the next instant she was freed, stepping nimbly back from him.

'You'll pay for that!' he bit out savagely. 'And next time you'll not escape, I swear it!'

'There'll not be a next time,' Gina assured him, pausing to look at him with disdain. 'You're a poor pathetic creature,' she said. 'I even think I pity you.' And as she turned and strode swiftly and with dignity away, up towards the house, she soon found that she wasn't as unperturbed and in control of the situation as she might have imagined. Tears slipped down her cheeks and the unsteady hands that wiped them away reflected the stress that was quaking in every limb and playing havoc with her nervous system.

She went through the front door, closed it quietly and leaned back against it, closing her eyes, feeling the wetness of her spiked lashes as they lay against her cheeks. As she stood there dabbing at her eyes on the cotton of her slip she wondered whether she should go and bid her parents goodnight or flee there and then to

the privacy of her bedroom. Becoming aware suddenly
of the murmur of voices, she straightened the skirt of
her dress and then tried to gauge from which direction
they came. From either the lounge or the dining-room,
she suspected, and on impulse decided to investigate. If
it was either of her parents she could let them know she
was off to bed.

However, as she drew nearer to the dining-room and
the voices became more distinct, she realised that they
belonged to neither parent but rather to Colette and—
Mitch! Heeding her instincts, she pulled back sharply,
refraining from entering the dining-room, and through
the door, slightly ajar, she could see the two of them
standing in the doorway to the lounge.

'What are you doing in here anyway?' Colette was
asking while at the same time sidling closer to him than
she was.

'I was looking for Gina,' Mitch replied, 'but it
doesn't appear as though she's in the lounge either.'

'Well, if she's not with Norrie then I'd say she's gone
to bed already. She's like that—quiet and moody. You
never know what's she's up to or what she's thinking,
while I . . .'

'While you are an open book,' Mitch finished for her.

Gina saw her sister pout up at him, looking at him
from beneath her lashes.

'Why worry about what Gina's doing? She's no fun.'
Colette had finally positioned herself so that she stood
directly in front of him with only a fraction of space
separating her body from his. The top of her head
barely came level with his heart and her long blonde
hair cascaded like a swathe of silk down her back as she
gazed up at him. 'Gina's always been a bit of a cold
fish. She'd never know how to appreciate a man like
you. Whereas I,' her head tilted to one side and the tip
of her tongue appeared at the corner of her mouth
while her small shapely hands slid up over the front of
Mitch's red shirt, unfastening several buttons in the
process, 'I know all there is to know about pleasing a
man like you.'

'Yeah, I bet.' Mitch's hands came up and caught her

roving ones and brought them down and away from him. 'Only you're a kid, and I don't accept invitations from kids—particularly spoilt, unscrupulous brats!'

The pink tongue tip disappeared and the bottom lip was jutted out, but the astounded Gina had a sudden revelation. There was no rancour in her sister's attitude, only feigned pique—plus a very real, raw kind of excitement.

'I'm twenty-three,' she told him.

'Like I said, you're a kid.'

'Mmm, but I can get into a man's blood like fire, they say.' She brought herself against him and ran her hands around his waist to trail her fingers lightly up his spine.

'More like poison, I'd say,' Mitch rejoined with a humour that made Gina cringe in humiliation for her sister.

But Colette appeared to be quite impervious to his insults. 'Let me prove it to you. Once you've had a taste of fire, I guarantee you'll never hanker after ice again . . .'

The voice suddenly lost its purring quality and broke off on a genuine howl of pain. And Gina herself started and took a step backwards, pressing a fist of knuckles against her lips as she witnessed Mitch wrench Colette's arms from around him and thrust them violently behind her back and hold them there.

'Dames like you are ten a penny on the streets where I come from,' he told her with grim humour, 'and the only fire they possess, I've found, is in their serpent's tongue. From my vast experience and youthful encounters with unsavoury types such as yourself, I've learned to do one thing extremely well and that is—to run like hell. As far as I'm concerned, sweetheart, your sister has more sex appeal in her little finger than you have in your entire misspent body.' He turned her about and gave her a shove that wasn't totally devoid of sympathy. 'Now, quit while you're ahead. Go find your heart's desire and leave me to look for mine . . .'

Her breath still suspended, Gina retreated hastily and made her way swiftly and silently to her room. She perched down on the end of her bed and for a long time her eyes, burning with tears she wanted but seemed unable to shed, stared sightlessly at the patterns the moonlight shining through the lace curtains was casting across the floor.

There was no doubting that this weekend would have to be one of the strangest of her entire life. The events contained in the past forty-eight hours had the power to turn her around so completely that she knew she would never be the same again. She was facing in a totally new direction where there was no assurance of security, no certainty any more of where her future lay, where the road led or what lay in wait for her. Nothing was as sure as it was this time last week, or at any time in the weeks and months that had preceded it during the past five years, and probably never would be again. The only positive sense she had was that there was no going back. And she gripped the edges of the mattress on either side of her in sudden panic. What *was* going to become of her?

She rose slowly and began to prepare for bed. On returning from the bath-room she found her mother waiting for her at the door to her room.

'Are you all right?' she asked. 'I was a little anxious about you when you disappeared so suddenly.'

Gina's smile was a little strained. 'I'm fine, Mum. I'm glad you came to find me. I wanted to say goodnight, but I honestly couldn't find the courage to face that lot out there again. Would you goodnight to Dad for me?' Gina grimaced. 'And Mitch as well, I suppose.'

Phoebe laughed and enfolded her daughter in a warm embrace. 'All right, dear, but I think Mitch will be disappointed. He's been looking for you.'

Gina shrugged. 'No doubt Colette will be glad to offer him consolation.'

'Gina!' her mother shook her head reprovingly. 'I don't know what it is you see when you look at Mitch, but I certainly wish it was what I see.' She sighed and patted her back. 'What time do you have to be away tomorrow?'

'Before lunchtime, I suppose. I hate having to leave,

Mum. That's the only disadvantage about coming home, is having to leave again.' Gina kissed her warmly. ''Night, Mum. I'm glad the party was such a success.'

Exactly what did her mother see when she looked at Mitch? Gina wondered as she lay wide awake, her thoughts darting and racing all over the place like mice in a maze. She groaned to herself and turned over, shifting her position yet again. She simply couldn't lie awake all night thinking about Mitch. The discovery and acceptance she had made of the fact that Colette and Norrie were indeed as alike and as suited to each other as Norrie had claimed was momentous enough in itself, as was the surprise she experienced when she came to admit that it didn't matter. Not one iota. They no longer had the power to hurt or to haunt her.

But Mitch's startling disclosure was another matter altogether, and one on which she had no wish to dwell.

She awoke suddenly from her fitful sleep and lay, her heart pounding, wondering whether the sound that woke her came from within her room. Fright licked along her nerves. Surely Norrie wouldn't . . . No. The sound came again—from Mitch's room. She sat up, listening closely. He was groaning—no, it sounded like sobbing, crying out as if in invocation.

She hesitated for a moment, then flung back the bedcovers. She reached for her housecoat and pulled it on as she made her way quickly and quietly along to his room. She spoke his name softly as she approached the bed on which he lay, twisting and twitching in sudden rather violent spasms.

'*No*! There are women and children . . . Oh, God . . .!'

Gina became rooted to the spot, poised and rigid, shocked by the anguish which distorted his voice beyond recognition. 'Mitch . . .?'

'Climb, you dumb bastard!' he pleaded angrily. 'For God's sake, climb!' and his impassioned voice evolved into a groan of frustration such as Gina had never heard before, so unparalleled, so agonising and all-consuming, that in a split second an intense heat had enveloped her entire body. Perspiration broke out over her skin which, for one second, was unendurably warm while the next it prickled as though the moisture had turned to ice.

Fear slithered through her. She wanted to clap her hands over her ears and flee, but she knew, as she had down at the gate with Norrie, which voice she had to obey. Moving forward, she felt for the switch of the bedside lamp and gazed apprehensively down at the sweat-soaked bedding on which Mitch tossed and turned, his head on the pillow wrenching first one way and then the other—a sight that only served to confirm that she had not the first idea how to handle this situation.

'Mitch!' she whispered intensely. 'Mitch!' This time she took a bare glistening shoulder and shook him until his eyes opened with such a suddenness, she started and stepped back. Like brilliant blue pools they stared up at her, glazed and momentarily uncomprehending. Then he startled her further by sitting bolt upright.

'What are you doing here?' he demanded, his voice thick with sleep. 'The barracks are no place for women.'

'Mitch,' she spoke softly and as calmly as she could. 'It's me, Gina. You're here at Tiraumea.'

Full consciousness dawned in a flash, and he frowned. 'What are you doing here?' he asked again.

'You were having a—nightmare,' Gina explained. 'Don't you remember? I heard you crying out and came to see—to see if you were all right.'

A split second before he rubbed a hand over his face, evidence that he did in fact remember the content of his nightmare was clearly visible in his expression. When he looked at her again, his expression was quite passive. 'I'm sorry for waking you. Go on back to bed now. I'm fine.'

'You're not fine, at all,' Gina contradicted mildly. 'Your sheets are saturated. Get up and I'll change them.'

'They're okay . . .'

'It won't take any time to remake your bed,' Gina cut in firmly. 'You can't sleep in those sheets.' And suspecting that he wore no pyjamas, she hoped he would take advantage of her momentary absence by slipping on at least the bottoms. This he did, and was tying the cord when she returned with a pair of clean sheets.

'Don't catch a chill,' she said, her glance skidding over his muscular chest and shoulders before she turned her full attention to stripping and remaking his bed.

'No, ma'am.'

And although she didn't look at him, she could detect the amusement present in his voice and marvelled to herself. There was no understanding him at all. Barely five minutes previously she had heard and seen him, his face and voice contorted with an agony wrung from the depths of a tortured soul, and now here he was behaving as though life was nothing but a joke! His ability in this respect perturbed her, nonetheless she worked at concealing her perturbation. When she had finished re-sheathing the pillows and had dropped them in place, she looked over at him. She wasn't surprised to find his eyes upon her, narrow, lazy, expressionless.

'What happened to you this evening?' he asked.

Gina shrugged carelessly. 'I went for a walk and then . . .'

'With Norrie?' he cut in.

'By myself. But believe what you like. Then I went to bed.'

'Without even saying goodnight?'

'I asked my mother to do that for me.'

'I thought first and foremost I was your guest.'

Gina opened her mouth to retort that Colette had more than made up for her in all areas in which he found her lacking. But then she recalled the scene she had caught fragmented glimpses of through the slit in the dining-room door and his ready defence of her, and the words become stuck in her throat. 'I'm-sorry,' she managed, lowering her eyes. 'This weekend has been quite—quite a strain for me. I've taken it out on you— used you again, and I apologise. But——' she lifted her eyes to his bravely and continued, 'although I know I don't show it, I do appreciate you having come with me this weekend.'

Mitch said nothing, for he had no need of words when his eyes could convey to her more than words ever could all of what it was he wanted her to know. Heat, the kind that only he had ever been able to ignite, spread over her skin and she felt robbed of breath, strength and almost of her very will. It was just so ridiculous to feel this way, she admonished herself, to bend under the force of his personality when on most occasions she found this man to be totally abhorrent to her. 'I hope you'll be able to sleep peacefully for the rest of the night,' she said stiltedly, succeeding in subduing the effects of this power he seemed able, at times, to exert over her, thus saving herself from a situation she decided it would be better to leave hidden and uninvestigated behind the curtains of her imagination.

Mitch said nothing.

'We'll probably be leaving late tomorrow morning and stop somewhere along the way and have lunch.' She stooped, gathered up the crumpled sheets and straightened once more, summoning from somewhere the courage to look at him. The desire in her to offer him comfort, ask if he needed to talk, a hot drink, anything at all, was strong, but she knew that something, a kind of change in the atmosphere between them, had eliminated what opportunity there might have been for her to display any care or concern.

Without another word she left him. After a long period spent deep in thought in the darkness of the laundry, she roused herself and was shocked to discover that she had spent the entire duration with her mouth pressed into the bundle in her arms. With an impatient murmur, she opened the lid of the automatic washing machine, thrust the sheets inside and returned to her room with a haste on which she refused to speculate.

CHAPTER SIX

WHEN Mitch offered the following morning to take the wheel for the first stint of their homeward journey, Gina didn't demur. Despite his disturbed night, he appeared refreshed and in high spirits and as usual was alert and charged with restless energy.

This was how he appeared to Gina when she went into the kitchen to find her mother preparing breakfast for him and her father, while the two men exchanged lively conversation that was punctuated liberally with bursts of robust laughter.

So the nightmare had had more of a debilitating effect on her than it had on him obviously, she observed, not without rancour. And she couldn't help remarking on the incident after they had said their farewells and were on their way.

'You look none the worse after last night,' she said.

'Unlike you, I enjoy parties.'

'I had noticed.' Gina couldn't refrain from shooting him a dry grin. 'But I was referring to your nightmare.'

'Oh, that.' Mitch pulled a face. 'It must have been something I ate.'

But although Gina was wise enough to permit him to shrug the matter off lightly, she didn't for a moment believe him. He was a strange man, she thought, staring at him with unmindful candour. An enigma. Funny how at the beginning she had dismissed him out of hand as being a clod, thick and stupid, dull. But although now she didn't think of him this way at all, she was left floundering, not knowing what to think.

'I won't get any prettier, unfortunately.'

'I beg your pardon?' Gina blinked uncomprehendingly.

'You're sitting there looking at me as though I was a frog you were hoping would turn into a handsome prince!'

Gina laughed so spontaneously, she surprised not only him but herself.

'Now that's a real nice sound. I don't think I've heard it before.'

Gina turned her head away, acknowledging to herself that it was a sound she hadn't heard much of herself, and it saddened her to realise just how much time she had wasted fretting, nurturing bitterness and bucking at the blow she considered fate had dealt her. When all the while fate, as Mitch had been swift to point out, had been nothing but kind . . .

'I thought you'd have an attractive laugh,' Mitch went on. 'You have a beautiful voice—when you're not snapping and snarling at me, that is. It has a husky quality which I think is kind of sexy—not to mention your prissy accent.'

Gina kept her face rigidly averted, feeling heat rush to accompany the surprise that became mirrored there.

'Now that I've said that, I hope you're not going to go all silent on me. I'll need you to talk to me to keep me awake.'

Her head swung back around at this. 'I thought you weren't tired. You seemed on top of the world first thing this morning.'

'Yes, well, I've learned over the years to survive on a few hours' sleep, but when a beautiful woman pays me a brief yet tantalising nocturnal visit, I find that I'm deprived even of those.' A short time later he slanted a glance at her and laughed. He reached for her right hand which was bunched inside her left one and pushed into her lap. Incapable of articulate speech, she put up a silent resistance, but his hand was far bigger and stronger than hers and conceding to the futility of her struggles, she allowed her hand to go limp and be drawn across to his leg where he pressed it, palm and fingers extending downwards, on to his hard lightly clad thigh. He gave it several gentle pats as if in an attempt to persuade her to leave her hand where he had placed it while he returned his own to the wheel.

Needless to say, her hand flew back immediately to rejoin the other while embarrassment seared her skin like a branding iron. 'When did you say you went back to the States?' Gina queried, hoping her voice sounded more evenly pitched to his ears than it did to her own.

Mitch laughed. 'Soon, honey. In about ten days.'

'Are you married?' she asked with an abruptness that stunned both of them.

'Why ask me a question like that now?'

'I don't know. I suppose because it never occurred to me to ask it before now. Well, are you?' she persisted when he remained silent.

'Do I act like a married man?' he shot her a look and from it, Gina gleaned that by her question she had somehow displeased him.

'No, but then the actions of a man quite often mean nothing.'

'Like Norrie's towards you?'

Gina shrugged. 'I wasn't thinking of anyone in particular, but if one needed an example to draw on then he would be as good a one as any.'

'Engaged to be married to you while all the time carrying on an affair with your sister behind your back.'

Gina cast him a brief glance and said dryly: 'Don't let those self-ordained omniscient powers go to your head. He wasn't quite that notorious.'

'Wasn't he?' And although his tone was neutral, Gina knew instinctively that his inference wasn't intended to be oblique. She looked at him and then away, and remembered, with barely suppressed shiver of trepidation, the sight of Norrie that morning as he had stood, aloof from her parents, Mitch and herself as they exchanged their farewells, his shoulder propped up against the verandah post and his eyes, slitted against the morning sun, resting unwaveringly upon herself. Another shiver ran over her and this time she felt as though her flesh had been chilled by a portentous ill wind.

'Your naïveté alarms me and I fear for your future.' Mitch's countenance darkened reflectively as he said: 'I wouldn't trust that slimy rat out of my sight.'

Gina remained silent, wishing fervently he would change the subject.

He shot a glance at her. 'What's this? No rushing to his defence? Don't tell me you've seen the chameleon in his true colours?'

She sighed impatiently. 'If you mean, have I found he no longer attracts me as he once did, then the answer is, yes. Now let's talk about something else. Did you see Colette this morning?'

'No. According to your mother she was still in bed asleep.'

'Well, I'm glad she succeeded where I failed last night.'

'What do you mean?'

'Just that she's like you in some ways and so was more able to entertain you than I. She likes flirting and parties.' Gina sighed within herself, Where was this line of conversation going to end? In trouble, no doubt. Why did she always feel compelled to spar with Mitch to deride and devalue his character?

'And after herself, that's about all she does like.'

'She liked you. I wonder where she learned to do the hula so well.'

'If it suited her purpose, your sister could summon the power to do anything well.'

Gina looked at him in feigned surprise. 'You sound as though you didn't like her—and yet you seemed to be enjoying yourself in her company.' She sighed. 'But then she's lovely, isn't she? Cute and cuddly as well as being well endowed with what it takes to attract the opposite sex.'

'In my opinion she has about as much sex appeal as a Barbie doll,' he said, 'and about as much in her head.'

Gina stared at him quite taken aback, for although his confirmation of what she had overheard him say the night before was what she had been angling for, she hadn't really expected to receive it. 'You surprise me,' she told him truthfully.

'Well, that doesn't surprise me. What you look for in people you meet is what your preconceived notions tell you should be there. But it's a mistake to categorise and earmark people and expect them to live up to the labels you put on them. Do you think I'm not aware that in your mind you've put me into a tidy little pigeonhole! Well, let me tell you, honey, there's not a pigeonhole invented by you or anyone else that will contain me, now or ever.'

Gina looked away from him and out at the forever changing countryside. She recognised the veracity of what he was saying and it was the first time she realised that she possessed such a trait and to have to accept this truth irked her. 'Don't call me "honey"!' she said irritably, in response to which he chuckled. 'You haven't yet told me whether or not you're married,' she accused him. 'You managed to skirt around that issue very nicely.'

'No, if I must spell it out to you, I'm not married.'

'Ever been?'

'No.'

'Why not?'

He quirked an eyebrow at her in amusement. 'By that question are you implying that you don't consider me totally ineligible?'

Gina made a grimace. 'I suppose there must be some women around who are attracted by your type—excuse the expression,' she added with mild sarcasm. 'I hope you won't immediately leap to the conclusion that I'm type-casting you again.'

'Some women, but not you, huh?'

'No.'

'Why not you?'

'You're just not my type. You're too—' too what? she searched her mind for one apt all-inclusive expression then gave up her quest and shrugged helplessly. 'Too everything—too peremptory, too volatile, too energetic and overpowering.'

'Perhaps it would take a woman to tame me. A woman like you.'

Gina ignored the inexplicable but definitely ridiculous thrill that darted through her at this softly spoken but wholly taunting challenge, and shook her head emphatically. 'I couldn't live the pace or the course that such a task would demand I follow. I'd be consumed in the process. Give me a quiet life.'

'And a man with water in his veins on whom you could happily waste yourself for the remainder of your life.' Mitch pulled off the road suddenly and into a layby sheltered by trees. 'I don't know about you, but I'm ravenous. Your mother packed us quite a lunch. Let's go and stretch out in a nearby paddock and eat.' He switched off the ignition.

Gina looked around her, saying a trifle dubiously, 'I think this is the only area that's not private property.'

'Honey,' said Mitch, inclining towards her and pocketing the keys, 'I've only ten days left in which to kindle in you that sense of adventure I'm willing to swear is lurking there somewhere. If I fail, I'm going to be very disappointed indeed.' And so saying, he swung himself out of the car and went around to unlock the boot.

Gina stood by and watched him as he tossed a rug over the fence, lowered the chillibin over the other side and turned to her. 'Are you coming, or do I feast on my own?'

Gina hesitated, opened and then closed her mouth, and finally shrugged in capitulation. Without a word, she crossed to the fence, climbed over, picked up the rug and followed where he led.

'Here's a good spot,' he said, setting down the chillibin and, with his eyes shielded against the sun, he gazed about him.

Their surroundings comprised near and distant hills, a slow-flowing river which curved and twisted along the floor of the valley that spread before them and cliffs which dropped down into it, sheer and white owing to the relentless process of corrosion. 'If the sun becomes too intense we can move farther under these trees.'

'I expect you're quite used to heat like this,' Gina remarked, shaking out the rug.

'Not so much of this dry blazing variety. It's usually more humid and sticky. I prefer it like this.'

'How do you live over there?' she asked, suddenly curious. 'Are you in barracks?'

'I was. But I bought a small bungalow just recently.'

Together they began unwrapping the food Phoebe

had painstakingly packed and transferring it on to the paper plates provided.

'I suppose you would get tired of living in such close proximity to other men, and having to forfeit your privacy?'

'Sometimes.'

'Do you hope to get married some day?'

'A soldier's a man without a woman—and that's the way it should be.'

Gina was puzzled by the sudden almost imperceptible cooling in his attitude, and the waning in his normally active inclination to converse. She had half expected to be met with a challenge similar to the one he had flung at her in the car. 'And that's the way you like it?' she asked.

'That's the way I like it.'

They ate in silence for a while and then, without prompting her, Mitch elaborated a little on his opinion on the subject. 'I've seen it constantly—experienced it too. Men and women professing to love each other, building one another up one minute, only to tear each other down the next. Look at your sister and her friend—not as extreme an example as you might think. Tearing each other apart, delighting to see the other reduced, humiliated, and then begin to put back the pieces bit by bit, stringing out the process, the exercise sating their morbid lust for power and control over another's life, another's emotions while at the same time appealing to their warped sense of magnanimity and depraved concept of love. God knows how, but I've managed to escape being trapped by such a destructive force, but not many of my buddies have been as fortunate.

'You don't agree?' he queried abruptly, attempting to interpret her silence.

'Yes—yes, I do, in some cases,' she began tentatively, still dazed by this glimpse of a facet of Mitch's character which, up until now, he had skilfully kept concealed. 'I agree you have a point. But on the other hand the friends I know have very successful marriages.'

He stared at her for a moment or two and then shook his head as though in self-disgust. 'What am I doing asking you this? As sheltered as a babe all your life, what could you possibly know?'

Her mouth opened to dispute this allegation, but then closed again as she accepted that, comparatively speaking, he was right.

'What made you decide on an Army career?' she asked tentatively, deciding the safest course would be to change the subject.

Mitch shrugged carelessly. 'It seemed a good idea at the time, besides looking like the only option open to me.'

'Do you like it?'

'That's a question I never consider. The Army's my life.'

'So will you go on eventually to become an officer?'

His eyebrows lifted on an angle and the look he slanted her way owned a quizzical gleam. 'Why this sudden interest in my affairs?'

Gina sat back on her heels and reflected a while and, as she fixed her pensive gaze upon him in the act of reaching for a tomato before lying on one side propping himself up on one elbow, his words to her of the night before came unbidden to her mind: 'I already know there's nothing about me that interests you.' 'I don't know,' she confessed slowly. 'Perhaps because I realise I don't know much about you. Will you go on and become an officer?' she asked again.

He kept his eyebrows on a slant. 'Was your father an officer?'

'No. But then he never intended making the Army his life.'

'So you think it automatically follows that because I've made the Army my life I should want to become an officer?'

Gina was bewildered by both his tone and his attitude. 'I don't know,' she said. 'You're confusing me. Am I asking all the wrong questions? I really don't know what questions to ask.'

He laughed humourlessly. 'Most women claim the

same thing, but strangely enough they all know to ask that particular one. Who do you think really runs the outfit? Keeps the wheels turning, the joints oiled, the men trained, paid and fed? The Captains and the Generals? You watch too many second-rate movies, honey, if you do. Without the Top Sergeants the companies would seize up. Without me, my company would grind to a halt.' His eyes were glowering at her and hers in turn became transfixed. 'Who do you think really knows how the insides work, who gets the Captain out of his jams, who comes up with the ideas and lets the Captain think they're his, who makes the decisions that need to be made, who knows what correspondence needs to be written and who writes it and blots the Captain's signature? Who steers his wife in another direction lest she discovers just to what extent the son-of-a-bitch she's married to is two-timing her? I like my stripes, I like to know first hand what's going on and being in control, even if it means letting the Captain believe he is. And further more, I like the company I keep, and as Top Sergeant I'm in a position whereby I can choose it. The air's maybe less rarefied and antiseptic down near my rung on the ladder, but to me it still sure smells a whole lot better than that circulating in the higher echelons.'

A lengthy silence followed, during which Gina grappled with her further shattered illusions and endeavoured to assimilate what he had been saying and wondered how to cope with the fragments of further smashed preconceptions. 'I—see,' she said at last.

'Do you?' Mitch gave a derisive snort of laughter. 'Ask your father if you don't think I'm giving it to you straight.'

'You—seemed to get on very well with Dad.'

'I did. He's a man after my own heart.' Mitch wiped his mouth and hands on a serviette and lay back on the brittle pasture, spurning the soft comfort of the rug.

He hadn't eaten much and Gina wondered whether he had had sufficient or whether their topic of conversation had been instrumental in causing him to lose his appetite. 'What did you find to do all day

Saturday?' she asked, continuing with her meal. 'You were gone the whole day.'

'Your father showed me over Tiraumea and the immediate vicinity. Apparently he'd like to concentrate more on fruit farming than dairy farming.'

'Yes. He's always had a flair for orcharding. I expect he showed you his kiwi-fruit vines? He's very proud of them.'

'And with good reason. He'd like to expand in this area, which would mean giving up the dairy side of the farm.'

'So he's been saying for years.'

'Does that fact make it any less true, his yen any less fervent?'

Gina's eyes widened at the strong hint of reproach in his voice. 'No, I didn't say that.'

'You know what it's like to have a dream you'd like to see eventuate into reality. You told me about it.'

'And Dad imparted his to you too?' Gina gave a brief laugh. 'You must have what it takes, to extract the cherished and secret dreams of the Wells clan!'

'Your father asked me if I'd like to purchase the dairy side from him?'

Gina choked on a mouthful of apple juice. The spate of coughing was not severe and she was soon able to expostulate: 'What on earth made him do that, for heaven's sake? What do you know about farming?'

Mitch turned a lazy blue gaze upon her. 'I told you I was brought up on a farm, didn't I? I thought I did.'

'Yes—yes, you did,' Gina admitted, recalling all of a sudden that he had mentioned something about a farming background, but she remembered also her own previous apathetic responses to much of what he had to say. 'But a farming background scarcely constitutes a farmer.'

'Right enough. But I worked on that farm as hard and as long as if it were my own right up until I was forced off it at twenty-one. And if I'm nothing else, I'm an excellent pupil, especially when experience is my teacher. There's nothing that goes in up here,' he tapped his head with a middle finger, 'that doesn't stay up here.'

'Why were you forced off the farm?' she asked. 'Didn't your parents own it?'

'I didn't have any parents. My mom died and my father's life was the sea. At the age of eleven, after running away from foster-homes so many times, I lost count, I went from the heart of New York City to the heart of the mid-West, and I knew that that was where I belonged. My uncle brought me up as though I were his own son. Except that I wasn't, of course, and he had a duty to remember that. My aunt died when I was fifteen and my uncle when I was twenty-one. He wanted to leave me the farm; he never said so, but I knew it. He couldn't, though, because he had three of his own sons. They were older than I and all went off to university and embarked upon careers that took them off the land. When the old man died, they sold it, and it damn near broke my heart.'

Gina sat, her arms linked around her knees, still and silent, her gaze trained upon his face that was upturned to the cloudless blue canopy overhead. Never had she felt so inadequate or at such a loss for a response.

Suddenly he laughed, a harsh laugh, devoid of his usual warmth and humour. 'Now what made me go and exhume that corpse? I thought it had been so long buried it would have been reduced to dust by now.'

'Do memories, happy or sad, ever turn to dust?' asked Gina.

'They should. There's hardly enough room for the present, let alone the past, and there's certainly no place for it.'

And as he spoke, she knew she had heard him say that very same thing the night before, but then she had been in no mood to appreciate that philosophy or any other observation or opinion he might have to make known. Now she realised that if he was ruthless in any one area, it was this one, of working at ensuring that the past remained in its rightful place and pressing on, progressing from one chapter in life to the next, though not before availing himself of their only worthwhile contribution—the lessons each experience taught him.

The silence that fell between them became stretched, much to Gina's relief. She had more than enough to mull over for the time being and she honestly doubted whether she could bear up if any more of the conclusions she had so carelessly arrived at about Mitch came toppling down on her. She darted a glance at him from beneath her lashes, and on discovering he had dropped off to sleep, she altered her position. Lying forward on her stomach, she supported herself on her elbows, rested her chin in cupped hands and so remained, studying him for some time. Then abruptly, as if baulking at the direction in which her thoughts were leading her, she sat up and began to pack away the scraps and left-over food. Once the chore was completed, she lay on her back and gazed up at the leafy shade of her umbrella until she too fell asleep.

When she came to it was with a start. Her eyes flew open suddenly and her mind was instantly alert, befuddled in no way by sleep, and when immediately encountering Mitch's blue steadfast gaze fully aligned with her own, she felt no surprise, only a swift but pleasurable shock. He had shifted his position and lay on his side next to her, and although no part of his body touched hers, it was as though they had never been this close before.

'I'm starving,' he murmured.

'I'm not surprised,' she responded mechanically, unable to tear her gaze from his as he loomed nearer. 'You didn't have much to eat.'

She didn't understand his smile, and then she abandoned all desire to try. She understood nothing about him, the present conflict going on in her feelings or the strange magic web that was settling over her, and all at once she didn't care if she didn't understand anything ever again. At the touch of his lips, warmed by the sun, firm, authoritative, closing over hers, everything in her seemed to surge in wonder, and that wonder welled up towards her throat as if demanding to be expressed in a soft gasp or cry of awe. But she remained silent and quite quite still as, with quickened breath, Mitch removed his lips from hers and they continued their slow sweet ministry up across her cheekbones, her eyes, her temples, along her nose and then her chin, and at no stage did he attempt to touch her or seal the gap that separated them. The sun infused her with warmth and a sense of wellbeing as she tilted her face and his lips glided along her jawline to her ear. She heard his breath being expelled on a deep suffocated moan which seemed to ricochet through her drowsily aroused senses. She turned her head jerkily, as if impelled even though afraid, to investigate his expression.

His slumbrous heavy-lidded gaze bored into hers briefly before he relaxed abruptly beside her and grinned. 'You have a dimple, did you know that?' Of course she did, but for some reason incomprehensible to her, she found herself shaking her head. 'When you smile, right here on the bottom of your chin.' The tip of his forefinger touched an area on the side of her chin bone. 'As well as an enchanting mouth.' His gaze lifted to rest upon it and his finger came to lie upon the corner nearest him. 'I guess I've told you that. I like the way it looks right at this moment. No longer stern or controlled but soft, inviting, made to yield to a man's kisses . . .'

'No. . . .!' Her protest was stifled and inarticulate as she turned away with the intention of rising. But Mitch's reflexes proved, as always, swifter than hers. This time he loomed over her more fully, although still his body made no significant contact with hers. Resting on his forearms, one on either side of her head, he lowered his mouth to claim hers even more assertively before. His lips moved persuasively, coaxing hers to part, which they did, for she had no practice in withstanding such expertise nor the blatant sweet sensuality which entered her blood, like a current of liquid honey. A current which seemed to meet and explode its target at the sweeping contact he made across the inside of her upper lip.

A split second later his head had lifted and he was on his feet, pulling her up with him. 'Time to hit the road, I think,' he said brusquely, and scooping up the rug he folded it roughly and thrust it into her arms.

Dazed and shaken, Gina brought her arms up automatically to receive it and fighting vainly to pull herself together and behave as though her senses hadn't in fact suffered a battering, she tried to emulate Mitch's composed matter-of-fact manner.

During the remainder of the journey, conversation between them was not resumed by Mitch, and since she felt no inclination to revive it, the trip was made in relative silence. Occasionally she found her gaze straying to his profile and had to make a concerted effort to control it which imposed further strain on her.

They arrived at the city's boundaries just as the sun was setting, and despite Gina's instructions to drive out to the camp so that he could be dropped off, Mitch ignored them altogether and without a word drove directly to her home. Did he expect she would invite him to stay to tea? She would like to have, but she sincerely doubted that she would be able to bear up under another minute, let alone another hour or two, of tension.

'I'm going into town for a while,' Mitch told her as he switched off the ignition. 'I'll help you carry in your gear and see that everything inside is in order.'

Gina thanked him in subdued tones and went on ahead of him to unlock the house. Indoors the air was warm, stuffy and mildly redolent of the perfume she used. She stood beside the kitchen table amid the lengthening shadows and realised that in two short days everything had changed. Nothing was the same nor ever would be again. What was she going to do?

She turned with a slight start as Mitch entered through the double quarter-paned doors and deposited her belongings on the floor. She stared at him with eyes that felt as large as grit-edged saucers. In two short months this large brash-sounding, coarse-looking American sergeant had turned her whole life upside down. What *was* she going to do? she wondered again.

'What's the matter?' he asked. 'You look as though you've seen a ghost!'

'I—I expect I'm just tired.' She made an attempt to smile. 'Would you—would you like to have something to eat before you go . . .?' She was still speaking when, to her horror, her vision blurred as without warning tears sprang to her eyes.

With a smothered exclamation Mitch was at her side and with rough tenderness pulled her into his arms. She was neither a short or a small girl, and yet she felt lost in him. A large hand came to rest against the back of her head and her face was pressed into the hard warm crevasse of his shoulder, and within this haven she wept and trembled until her tears ceased and her trembling restricted itself to the inner core of her being.

'It's been a hell of a weekend for you, I guess,' came his gruff sympathetic tones, obviously oblivious to the fact that he, more than Norrie, had been responsible for the hell in which she had and still did find herself. He had systematically torn down and destroyed the roof, the walls and even the very foundations of her security, her protective dwelling, leaving her utterly exposed without plan or direction. What *was* she to do?

'But now you're free,' he encouraged her. 'Free at last. And you've got a lot of making up to do.' He stroked and patted her hair as he spoke and then, taking the sides of her head between his hands, looked down into her face and as his eyes stared down into hers, made almost translucent by her tears, the expression in his underwent a change, as did the tenor of their embrace. His sharp indrawn breath seemed to hiss through his teeth and her mouth opened on a soundless cry as his fingers threaded through and tightened in her hair, tugging back her head.

Then suddenly she was free, and before she had had time to pull herself together, Mitch had reached the door and had turned to say briskly: 'I won't stay. I'll eat in town.'

'You will—you will come to dinner one evening before you leave, won't you?' Gina reached down to grip for support the back of one of the wooden chairs.

His smile was fleeting and somehow mechanical. 'Sure, I'll look in to say goodbye. I'll bring some champagne for you to celebrate.'

'Celebrate what?'

'I'll finally be out of your hair and you'll be able to relax and sink back into your nice safe predictable rut with no loutish unrefined uncultured Army sergeant around to haul you out. That'll be an occasion to celebrate, won't it?'

Gina remained exactly where she was for quite some time after Mitch had left. The confusion within her was rife, but the longer she reflected on what could be the cause, the more it seemed to elude her. She unpacked her small overnight case and decided to have a shower and wash her hair before preparing herself something to eat. Perhaps if she was refreshed she would be able to think more clearly.

However, four days and at least as many showers later, she was no nearer comprehending the sudden upheaval, almost reversal of her feelings for a man who had, up until that Sunday afternoon, possessed not even one attribute that she would have described as attractive, not one facet of his appearance or personality that would have endeared him to her.

When Mitch rang on Thursday evening at the end of the hottest day recorded so far for that year and suggested that they drive out to the beach for a swim, Gina hesitated, seized by a peculiar mingling of apprehension and excitement. While her common sense tried to influence her to suggest that they exchange their farewells over the phone and thus choose for herself a safe-rather-than-sorry option, something quickening her blood urged more softly, more insidiously to cast her caution to the winds.

'This is the last evening I'll have the car,' Mitch was telling her, 'so we might as well make use of it,' and obviously intending not to take no for an answer, he went on: 'I'll pick you up at seven.' And he rang off.

Throughout the drive out to Himatangi, neither of them spoke. An occasional glance at his profile told Gina that he was in a sombre pensive mood and for this she felt only relief. Her thoughts were too chaotic and her breath too restricted to carry on what would have to pass as a normal conversation. Her awareness of him was so foreign to her and yet so acute she found her

glance capable only of skimming over the bare
muscular legs beside her own, the brightly coloured and
highly patterned shirt she so abhorred and the strong
brown arms extended and hands competent and relaxed
on the wheel.

The beach was wide and clean, stretching on either
side of them for as far as the eye could see. Even the
view of the ocean and the vast horizon was completely
uninhibited. The sun was lowering steadily, slipping
behind the gathering of cloud, and already there was
evidence of what promised to be a spectacular sunset.
At any other time during the previous weeks, Gina
would have made some quip, daring Mitch to tell her
that a Hawaiian sunset could surpass one such as this,
but the atmosphere between them seemed too tensed,
too charged for such banalities.

The sea proved not as mild as it looked, nor as warm
as one might have expected, and although Gina found
swimming through and with the waves considerably
invigorating, the cold chased her out long before it did
Mitch. She sat on the beach and waited for him, drying
off in the last of the sun's rays while watching the scant
numbers swimming, and farther along the beach buggy
and go-cart enthusiasts and beyond, still farther, the
lone fisherman, standing on the shore.

Gina stood on one side of the car while Mitch dried
and changed on the other. Beneath the soft folds of her
muslin caftan, she stripped off her bikini and reached
into her beach bag for her articles of underclothing—
only to find none. To her chilling dismay she realised
there was nothing she could do but accept that she had
left them behind, and the frantic groping of one hand,
then the other, ceased. They were probably still on her
bed where she had tossed them ready to·be packed
along with her towel.

She dropped the beach bag and stood paralysed with
indecision. One glance at her wet bikini revealed it to be
coated in sand.

'Ready?' came Mitch's voice.

'Y—yes.' She struggled into the caftan and thrust her
arms into the billowing sleeves. She would just have to

trust to luck that Mitch would pay her as scant attention on the way back as he had done on the way there. She looked down at herself. Perhaps the muslin wasn't as diaphanous as she supposed, and besides— she glanced at the gold horizon and the crimson glow extending like a fan across the sky—it would in all probability be dark by the time they reached her home.

The sunset's fiery glow was their companion for half of the twenty-mile return drive and then darkness stealthily crept into its place, and Gina was glad of it.

'Have you heard anything from Norrie since you've been back?' Mitch asked after escorting her to the door and entering, taking it for granted that she would invite him in.

Gina looked at him in surprise, but in the darkness was unable to see his face in detail. 'Of course not! What reason would he have to contact me?'

'None that you might be able to think of. I could think of several.'

'What—at *are* you doing?' Gina asked, even though she could see quite clearly what he was doing. Forgetting her state of dress, she moved towards the light- switch, but was forestalled by Mitch's hand clamping firmly around her forearm.

'I've taken off my shirt. I know how it offends you.'

'Then why wear it in the first place?' she demanded, suddenly experiencing a desperate need for more air.

His chuckle was deep and self-mocking. 'Why go for an ice-cold dip when all I want is to make violent, passionate love to you?' He took her wrist and drew her with him into the lounge, and there was no will or strength in her to resist him.

The soft shaggy pile of the carpet was the first awareness she had that it was the floor and not the settee on to which he was lowering her, and the raw primitive sensuality she sensed in both him and their situation excited even while it appalled her. Her pitiful murmur of protest died on her lips as this time the hard heavy length of him claimed contact with her and came to bear down upon her and his mouth began a thorough, in earnest exploration of each feature. Her heart struggled like a sparrow captured between two hands while her trapped frozen body gradually thawed and yielded with small restless movements in response to the insistent pressure of his.

The birth of a strange ache somewhere deep within her seemed to be convincing her that she couldn't get close enough to his man who had so recently and so utterly repelled her, and her hands, which had once shirked from all contact with him, slid up over his muscled back, now gloried in the hard smooth warm feel of him. When his mouth finally ceased the teasing of first her upper and then her lower lip and besought and plundered hers, shaking, it seemed, her very soul, it occurred to her to wonder fleetingly whether her need for this particular and prolonged contact was more desperate than his. Her murmur of protest when his mouth was removed from hers turned immediately to a sigh as the pressure of his lips lowered to the sensitive hollow beneath her ear and those of her throat and neck.

He rolled slowly on to his side, bringing her thigh over the outside of his own while keeping her hips sealed against his with hands that eventually moved up over the length of her back, the indentation of her waist and finally the curve of her breast. His breath, as hers had, caught, and his hands became still. 'My God!' he exclaimed thickly. 'Haven't you got anything on under this thing?'

Gina shook her head, the electrifying touch of his hands binding her power of speech and paralysing all sense beyond her ability to feel.

Mitch became quite still for a minute and it was as if he had stopped breathing. Then he uttered softly: 'Goddamn it! *Goddammit!*' The latter emerged like a muffled groan of mingled pain and rage. He wrenched himself away from her and hauled himself to his feet.

'Mitch!' Gina sat up, the huskiness in her voice more pronounced than even she had heard it.

He remained with his back to her for several moments and then turned on her as if in fury. 'Listen, honey,' he said harshly; 'in less than a week I'll be back on U.S. soil, and I don't want to arrive home after one night with you that will sure as hell leave me hankering for more and then begin tearing my guts out when I don't get it. Alcohol, I've discovered, is the only palliative, and the last time I got good and drunk over a woman was a damn long time ago, and I don't aim to get myself hitched up to that bandwagon again, now or ever. I'll call you.'

And with that he was gone, leaving Gina dashed and in a turmoil, too bewildered to cope alone with the barrage of emotions he had unearthed in her and left exposed and rejected. As if it was she who was wholly and solely responsible for the conflagration that had erupted between them.

Once her blood, surging so hotly only minutes before, began to cool and her clamouring senses accepted that their desire for fulfilment was to be denied them, another condition established itself within her, strange, foreboding, bleak. As though she had died and looming ahead of her was the onerous task of being born and learning to live all over again. She lay back on the floor and allowed silent unidentifiable tears to slip down, run over her ears and fall silently on to the carpet.

CHAPTER SEVEN

FIVE days dragged slowly by and Gina came to accept that Mitch had left without contacting her again, and she found she was almost relieved at having arrived at this conclusion. It meant she would no longer need to wait, perpetually on tenterhooks, for him to ring or call. She could begin to pick up the threads and get her life back into some semblance of order. It had taken a long time to get over the love she had had for Norrie—but then that, regardless of how she might feel about him now, had been love. What she had felt for Mitch had been a momentary, albeit powerful, flare-up of sexual attraction. She knew her confusion as to why or how she could possibly feel for Mitch that which she had always considered 'animal passion,' might always be with her, but this hitherto latent side of her sexual make-up would quickly die, never to be resurrected again. She couldn't afford to entertain doubts about that!

Had she really murmured his name over and over as her involuntary recollections kept insisting she had? she wondered as she curled up on her couch, her attention straying continually from the paperback copy of *The Silmarillion* resting at an angle on her lap. Her face grew hot as her memory worked on with a relentless activity that was eventually and effectively stemmed by a sharp rapping on the door.

Her heart gave an initial wild traitorous bound of expectation before being subdued cruelly by the realisation that the knock had been on the front and not the back door. And had it indeed been Mitch, he would have invited himself in before this.

Gina tucked her baggy-styled cream shirt more securely into the waistband of her violet-coloured skirt as she padded barefoot into the hall. Upon opening the door a spasm of sheer disbelief, by no means pleasurable, passed through her. Time seemed to stop as she stared at her visitor in incredulous silence. Then she obeyed her first impulse, even though she knew full well that to give in to the panic swift to rise in her would be a mistake. It was. Norrie's foot was thrust beside the jamb and the door slammed uselessly up against it. His weight sent the door crashing back on its hinges, compelling Gina to retreat hastily. With arms held rigid at her sides, she stared at him, struggling to regain her lost colour and composure. 'What are you doing here?' she got out between lips which all of a sudden felt stiff and dry.

Norrie stared at her, a mocking little smile playing on his lips. His eyes slid insolently over the length of her as he kicked the door shut behind him and their expression, or perhaps lack of expression, sent a piercing shiver right through her. 'What kind of welcome is that,' he asked smoothly, 'for your old love?'

Instinct was warning Gina that strategy was going to be her only ally in this situation, but premonitory fear had her wits so petrified she doubted her ability to employ any. 'Haven't you heard the dictum, off with the old?' she asked with a valiant attempt at flippancy, turning to re-enter the lounge.

'And on with the new, eh? Is that bragging Yank an example of "the new"?' Norrie followed slowly behind her, his hands in the sloping pockets of his short unzipped beige polyester jacket.

Gina stared at him in stony silence.

He gazed around him, his bland face taking on an expression of appreciation. 'You've done very well for yourself, by the looks of things—apart from that Yank. I'd have thought you'd have done better than him—a woman like you.'

'Since my slumming days with you, there was only one way for me to aim, and that was higher—and I did!' she shot back recklessly, and again the curious expressionlessness of those topaz eyes warned her that she wasn't dealing with any element here with which she was even remotely familiar.

'If being a soldier's groundsheet is your idea of promotion, then I'd say we still have a whole lot going for us.'

Gina's eyes formed diamond-bright. 'Get out!' she ordered without raising her voice.

Norrie laughed unpleasantly. 'Don't tell me you're still a prude. God, what a bore! A hypocritical prude is even worse than a virginal one. What was it about the American that captured your fancy? He's about as refined as a jungle primitive at a tea-party.'

'I've told you—he's a man! Which is a great deal more than can be said for you!'

'And which is an impression I've come for the express purpose of rectifying.'

Gina felt the distinct prickle of ice-cold perspiration break out over her skin, and the blood in both her hands and feet seemed to have frozen in an instant.

'Before this night's over you're going to find that he and I have quite a considerable amount in common in that respect.'

Frantically, Gina fought to prevent herself from slipping into the ever-widening quagmire of panic. She shrugged with simulated nonchalance. 'Stay, then, if you must. Only don't expect Mitch to behave too sympathetically towards you when he arrives.'

Norrie's eyebrows rose. 'When, tonight?' he queried, betraying no sign that he was worried.

'Of course tonight!' she retorted without hesitation.

Unexpectedly he laughed, a brief sinister sound. 'Good try, but don't make the mistake of taking me for a fool. I happen to know your hero returned to Hawaii yesterday—I made enquiries. Why do you think I delayed so long paying you this visit?'

For a few agonising seconds, Gina was certain she was about to pass out. The truth of what Norrie said registered with her like the impact of a fist slamming viciously into her solar plexus, and she was totally incapable of disguising her anguished reaction.

'You didn't know he'd left?' Norrie asked in genuine astonishment, then threw back his head and laughed in such a way that Gina wanted to clap her hands to her ears to block out the sound.

'Well, well,' he said, sobering. 'It seems as though he and I have more in common than I thought.'

'Get out!' Gina hissed at him, pointing to the door. 'Get out this instant or I'll call the police!'

Norrie responded merely by grinning at her, his eyes holding hers as he stripped off his jacket and dropped down into a nearby chair. 'Now don't let's have a display of histrionics—I have more of that than I can handle from Colette. And while you may be sisters, you're as unalike as night and day, and I've decided I'd like a little taste of what it was I walked out on. Besides, we have a little score to even up, you and I, if you'll remember. I don't like being kneed in the groin, so I'm afraid you're going to have to pay for that . . .'

As he spoke, Gina became suddenly very sure that no stratagems, however brilliant, were going to deliver her from this situation. It was as if the Norrie she had known, or even thought she had known, was no longer inhabiting this frame, and whoever his replacement was, or the person he had of his own will chosen to become, was someone from whom she wished to run as fast as her legs would carry her.

She made it only to the lounge door before she was caught from behind by the hair. She cried out, but Norrie's grip didn't slacken. Instead, with a ruthlessness which seemed to afford him some macabre form of satisfaction, he wrenched her back and around, pulling her head back until tears of pain slid from the outer corners of her eyes. She closed her lips tightly against his savage assault on her mouth. Revulsion shuddered through her and she could no longer retain her panic. She fought and struggled like a wild thing, desperation making her impervious to pain. She must have cried out for Mitch, because she heard Norrie give a breathless chuckle, quite devoid of humour. She saw him looking down at her, his face flushed and contorted by the grimness of his smile. 'Mitch won't be coming to your aid, my lovely. He's thousands of miles away, remember.'

The taunt wrung from her a cry of frustration. She wrested one arm from manacles formed by his hands, brought it up and managed to pummel his face with her fist only twice before he caught her wrist and, with his face a cold untenanted mask, reached out deliberately and slapped her before shoving her towards the couch. 'I don't prefer to use force on you,' he told her in a voice low and surprisingly controlled as his body pressed down on hers, 'but I will, so help me, if you don't start showing a little more co-operation. The choice is yours.'

The torture of being unable to escape his kisses went on, kisses which not only revolted but appalled her, and when his hands embarked upon a task of ripping away her already torn clothing, she became distraught. Sobs tore past her throat as she felt the last of her strength ebb away, and she lay unable to muster even the will to dig the nails of her now unshackled hands into his face.

Of what happened next she was only vaguely aware. There came the sound of a crash from somewhere, she knew that, but whether it came before or after she had been suddenly, gloriously freed, she couldn't and would never be able to tell. All that concerned her was that she was free. The weight of odious flesh had been lifted and the feverish movements of violating hands had ceased. Overwhelming relief flooded her being, finding expression in further tears. She turned on her side and drew herself up into a ball and cried until she was spent.

Some indeterminable time later a hand touched her shoulder, and for all its tentativeness she was in no frame of mind to recognise such an element in the touch of anything or anyone, and her reaction was swift and violent. She turned and reared to her feet, lashing out wildly with flailing arms and fists, furious sounds emitting from low in her throat.

'Gina! Cool it, Gina. It's me—Mitch.' And arms, more solid and thickly muscled than those that had not long before abused her with their superior strength, closed around her and held her tightly, their ambition only to impart comfort to her.

The accent and timbre of his voice penetrated her senses and brought her back to rationality. She became abruptly still and silent. Then, with a sob of one who had been rescued from a fate worse than death, she crumpled against him and with fingers closing over fistfuls of his shirt, she clung to him until her trembling ceased and he eased her gently away from him. His eyes, dark and pent, so unlike the eyes she knew so well which were blue as sunlit waters and always twinkling with ready laughter, searched her face. His hands came up to form a gentle frame. 'What did he do to you?'

Gina shivered convulsively. She had never heard him use this suppressed tone before, nor look so pale, so dangerous and capable of violence. There had been times, she knew, when she hated his perpetual good humour, and now she would have given anything to see it. 'Nothing . . .'

The hands cupping her ears and sides of her face,

tightened fractionally. 'Your clothes are in tatters, your face is swelling and discolouring. What did he do?'

'He—he forced his way in, th-that's all,' Gina stammered. 'He was—going to force himself on me, b-but you came ... Where were you? He told me you'd gone!' she cried, fresh tears welling into her eyes, as she moved of her own volition back into the haven of his arms and they closed about her as he muttered a heartfelt imprecation.

Some time later, he held her back from him and a fleeting glimmer of humour lightened his eyes as again he scanned her features. 'I've come to the inevitable conclusion that there's only one solution for the likes of you and me. We need someone to look after us and save us from the dubious comforts of our careers and a lonely old age. I think we should get married.'

As he spoke Gina experienced the most peculiar sensation. It was as if someone else in her was listening to his proposal and that someone else who nodded and gave him an affirmative response.

He looked at her closely, his eyes narrow, concealing the true nature of his thoughts. He reached down and in a matter-of-fact manner took an edge of the torn material of her blouse and brought it up to cover her breast, tucking it into the lacy edge of her bra. 'I think what you need is bed and a hot toddy.'

Gina flushed painfully, but again she agreed and with her hand automatically maing doubly sure the material was secure and concealing, allowed him to lead her to the bathroom where he proceeded to run a bath and then fill the handbasin with warm water. Taking a flannel and rinsing it in the water, he began bathing her face, gently and thoroughly, concentrating on the tender areas of her eyes and mouth.

As she silently submitted to his ministrations, a strange ache began to take root in her heart and spread to the lower regions of her body until she felt almost totally engulfed. She recognised the feeling for what it was, caught her breath and quickly lowered her eyes lest he should see written there this incredible unexpected yearning to submit to him in a greater, more complete way than this.

'What did you do to your hands?' she asked huskily, suddenly noting as he rinsed the flannel the fresh abrasions across his knuckles.

Mitch didn't so much as glance at them as he answered. 'I gave that rat a lesson he won't forget in a hurry.'

'Norrie? Wh-where?'

'Out in the back garden.' His mouth set grimly. 'I should have killed the bastard!'

'No . . .' In concern, Gina took one of his hands to inspect the extent of the injuries, but Mitch pulled free and went over to inspect the temperature of the bath water. 'I'm not unused to sporting a few cuts and grazes,' he said. 'Now have yourself a bath and I'll fix you something that will ensure you get a good night's sleep.'

She caught his arm as he made to leave her, looking up at him anxiously. 'You—you won't leave me here—on my own . . .?'

'No,' he said, gently patting her hand. 'I have no intention of doing that.'

'I thought—I really did think you'd gone, left without saying goodbye,' Gina told him as she sat up on her bed in her nightgown and housecoat, pushing the light covers back with her toes and sipping the toddy he had laced quite liberally with brandy. A lump had arisen and become lodged in her throat, making it painful to talk.

Mitch manoeuvred himself into a relaxed position on the end of her bed and from there his stare never left her. 'I was supposed to have flown out with the rest of the Company yesterday, but last-minute orders would have me spend a further three weeks in New Zealand, up at a place called Waiouru.'

Gina smiled at his surprisingly good pronunciation of the name.

'Which was just as well,' he went on sombrely, 'because I had no intention of leaving the country until I knew for sure that Freeman had left first.'

Gina's eyes widened. 'What do you mean?' she asked,

mystified. 'How would you know when he left or even if he intended to leave? Colette was thinking of staying in New Zealand.'

'I've been keeping in touch with your folks. They told me that Freeman and your sister had made reservations to fly out from Auckland two days ago. Your sister was on that plane, but not Freeman. I was in Waiouru yesterday and couldn't get away. I rang you last night, but you weren't home. I deliberated on whether I should keep trying until I reached you no matter how late, but I began to tell myself to relax. I was becoming paranoid over the guy. I neither liked nor trusted him, but that was no cause to suspect him capable of some heinous crime. But I was right all along. He's a mean and vicious character. I should have obeyed my former instincts and got here the moment I arrived back from Waiouru and not gone back to camp to get showered and sweet-smelling—then I could have saved you from all this,' he added the latter through teeth being brought in self-aimed anger.

Gina's vision of him blurred a little and impetuously she leaned across and slipped a hand into his. 'Don't flagellate yourself. You got here, and that's the main thing. You were checking up on him while he was doing the same as regards you. You don't know how I felt when he said you'd left!'

The corners of his mouth depressed in a grimace of faked humility. 'And to think that all the time I was under the impression you couldn't wait to see the back of me!'

She made to withdraw her hand, swift to leap to her own defence. 'I didn't want to see the back of you without being given the opportunity to say goodbye first.'

His grip on her hand tightened, thwarting its escape. 'Drink your toddy,' he indicated to the mug with a nod of his head.

A small stirring of excitement began in the pit of her stomach. She finished the remainder of the liquid with haste she was soon to discover was unwise. Mitch took the empty mug from her, placed it down on her bedside table and brought himself slowly up to lie beside where she sat. She didn't resist, but allowed him to draw her down until she lay against him within the warm strong shelter of his arms, feeling for all the world as though she had been created to fit there. The room began to revolve slowly, round and round, growing gradually dimmer. A hand stroked her, soothing, lulling her. She turned her face and obeyed a drowsy impulse to press her lips to the skin exposed between two buttons and the two strained edges of his shirt. His reaction was spontaneous, but apart from the brief almost compulsive slipping of his hand to her lower back and the increased pressure of his hips against hers, she fell asleep on a sigh and knew nothing more.

She awoke early the following morning and upon remembering the events of the night before wondered if the subconscious realisation that she was alone had woken her so sharply and with a sense of loss. A glance at her alarm clock told her it was half past five, and in normal circumstances she would have drifted back off to sleep. But something was telling her that even if Mitch hadn't lulled her to sleep in his arms the night before, these would not have been normal circumstances, and it wasn't until she had washed and dressed that she remembered, or at least suspected she remembered, why. Had Mitch in actuality suggested they marry, and if so, had she really said yes? Or had she in fact dreamed most of what she was now recollecting?

The early morning sun spilling through the kitchen's quarter-paned windows was not yet high enough in the heavens to reflect off the stainless steel bench and dazzle the eyes. Gina stopped short in the doorway, her heart contracting oddly as she saw Mitch seated at the kitchen table with a coffee mug beside him and the newspaper of the night before spread out in front of him.

He glanced up, his assessment of her swift and casual. 'You're up early—or do you normally rise at this hour?'

'I awoke suddenly and then I found I couldn't go back to sleep.'

'Miss me, huh?'

To her mortification her memory chose that moment to remind her of the kiss she had pressed to his chest, and colour stole up into her face. 'I—couldn't remember whether or not I'd dreamed all that happened last night.' She shrugged and hoped it would appear as nonchalant as she intended. 'I see I didn't. You're here as large as life.'

'How are you feeling?'

'I'm fine. That toddy you mixed packed quite a punch,' she said, hoping he would glean her intended meaning. 'I hope you didn't waste too much of my best brandy.'

'If it wasn't for the brandy,' he said drolly, 'I doubt whether either of us would be up at this hour. I was imagining you'd be grateful for the respite it provided.'

Gina's head swivelled round. She had crossed to the bench for the purpose of filling the electric kettle and was momentarily sidetracked by the implication behind his words. 'What do you mean—"respite"?'

His bland face told her nothing, but the expression in his direct blue gaze possessed a strange significance. 'What do you think I mean?'

Deciding abruptly that this hedging and hinting between them had to stop and that the matter had to be brought out into the open and the situation rectified before misunderstanding had a chance to arise, she quickly filled the kettle, plugged it into the hot point and turned to face him. 'Did you ask me to marry you last night?'

'Can't you remember?'

'I can remember several things very clearly. What I can't decide is what was dreamed, if anything, and what was reality.'

'I did suggest we get married, yes.'

'What on earth for?'

'I told you why.'

'But we have absolutely nothing in common.'

'On the contrary, we have everything going for us. And you must have thought so, or else you wouldn't have said yes—you hadn't imbibed at that juncture.'

'No, but I had been extremely upset. It was hardly

fair of you to take advantage of my emotional state.'

Mitch shrugged. 'Okay, if that's how you see it I'm willing to allow you to retract your acceptance. My offer of marriage, however, still stands, and I'd like you to consider it seriously. I think we should go ahead and apply for the licence, and if you decide to accept, we can be married before I leave in three weeks' time.'

'In three weeks' time!' she echoed, looking at him aghast. 'Do you mean you expect me not only to decide, but if my answer is yes, to marry you, all within three weeks?'

His look was one of insouciance. 'You're going on twenty-eight. I'm thirty-five. Surely we're mature and realistic and adult enough to know what it is we want in a partner, what ingredients go into making a successful marriage. I think we could not only be compatible lovers but be loyal and true to each other and provide one another with good company and friendship. You're opening and closing your mouth like a landed fish,' he added.

'Yes—well, at least now I know what a landed fish must feel like,' Gina retorted when she finally located her voice. Turning, she fumbled with the tea caddy and tipped more of the tea on to the bench than into the pot.

'Why are you so agitated?' Mitch asked calmly, observing her unco-ordinated movements.

'If you don't know, I'm blowed if I'm going to tell you!' she all but snapped, searching the cupboard beneath the bench and on sighting the toaster, realised what it was she was looking for. 'Do you want some toast?' she turned to ask ungraciously. 'Or have you already helped yourself to something to eat,' she tacked on, knowing full well he hadn't.

His expression became bodeful. 'Don't stand there throwing out blatant innuendoes about my helping myself. I could have helped myself to a damn sight more than I have. You'd be well advised to dwell on that.'

Gina looked quickly away from him and in silence began to cut slices from the wholewheat bread. She didn't need any time to dwell on his allusion. She knew full well what he was implying, and the truth of his claim witnessed to her somewhere deep down in her soul. Yet still the conflict continued between her indignation at the enormity of his egotistical assumption and shame at her bellicose attitude when she had to acknowledge she owed him so much.

She poached him two eggs, fried several rashers of bacon and one halved tomato, hoped it was what he would consider a sufficient breakfast, and set it down before him. 'Why are you up so early?' she asked in a modulated voice as they began to eat.

'I don't need much sleep. I had to learn to do without it and now I find I need only five hours, six at the most.'

'Why did you have to learn to do without it?' She looked at him curiously. Mitch shrugged. 'For one reason or another,' he said evasively.

'You don't seem to sleep well at all, do you?' she commented, remembering his disturbed night at Tiraumea.

'I'm looking forward to you changing all that for me once we're married,' he told her with a puckish tilt to his brows.

Gina fought to keep heat from staining her face with colour, but she must have failed to some extent, because he laughed, soft mocking laughter that irritated her immensely.

'Your reactions don't vary much, do they? I know exactly what to say to get you to blush like a virgin!'

Gina felt like swooning with relief when, being aware of his scrutiny, she managed to betray no reaction to this barb. 'How monotonous for you,' she sympathised sarcastically. 'You should be thinking yourself fortunate I did retract my acceptance of your proposal.' She rose, stacked their dishes and carried them to the sink.

'There's another reason why I want you to marry me,' he said abruptly as she stood with her back to him, pouring the tea.

Sensing he was about to say something momentous, she tensed and her grip tightened on the handle of the teapot.

'I'm in the throes of adopting a child, a little girl.'

Mitch paused as if waiting for a reaction from her. Receiving none, he continued: 'She's three years old and half-Vietnamese.'

Gina set down the tea-pot and turned with the two cups and saucers in her hands and set them down carefully on the table. She sat down and looked at him, deliberately ensuring that her face betrayed in no way the extent of the shock he had given her. Her mind raced, but it was instinct that made her to resolve to tread circumspectly and not prompt or question him. He should voluntarily tell her all that in the circumstances he considered she needed to know.

'You're not interested?'

'Of course I'm interested, as any woman would be, but not in the same way as one who was about to be married to you.'

'No other woman will do,' he told her quietly.

Gina looked down at her hands clasped loosely about the base of her cup. 'I'm sorry.' She went on after a time of silence: 'Does the lack of a wife preclude you from adopting the little girl?'

'Her name's Kim-Lan, and no, my marital status has no bearing in this instance. As at this moment she's in Saigon, and I'll move heaven and hell if necessary to get her out.'

Gina had never heard such intensity in his voice before. Her gaze lifted and became riveted on his face.

'Such drastic measures might not be necessary,' he continued. 'My application to sponsor her is going through without any hitches—so far.'

'What—what about her mother?' she asked diffidently.

'Her mother's dead.'

'And—her father—he's American, I take it?' she found herself asking, her resolution crumbling.

'Yes.' His voice harsh and expression bleak.

Was he the father? Her urgent need to know pushed her to the very brink of asking this forbidden question. And if so, had he been in love with the Vietnamese woman who had borne him a daughter? But her lips pressed firmly closed on countless questions she knew she would never ask. As she watched him, she felt an unaccountable sinking sensation somewhere in the region of her heart. Why else did he look so faraway, so tortured, as if reliving their times together and ultimately their parting? Had he tried to get her and the child out before Saigon fell? Had he tried to arrange their escape, only to fail . . .?

She opened her mouth, about to ask him if he had been in Vietnam, and realising such a question would be tantamount to asking these very questions, rephrased her wording, asking gently: 'Is Vietnam where you had to learn to make do with less sleep?'

He looked at her blankly for a second or two and then a glimmer of laughter introduced life back into his eyes. He straightened and stretched, then brought his arms down and the knuckles of one forefinger over the tip of her nose. 'Among other things,' he replied insinuatingly, and laughed when, in confusion, her gaze shied from his.

'Are you never serious for any longer than two minutes at a stretch?' she exclaimed crossly.

'If I were, honey, I'd be in a straitjacket.' He pushed back his chair and stood up, looking at his watch. 'I'm due back at base.'

Gina rose and walked with him to the door and out on to the sheltered brick patio. 'Thank you, Mitch. For what you did for me last night . . .' As she spoke a horrendous thought struck her and she looked up at him, her fingers clutching suddenly at his arm. 'He won't come back, will he?'

Mitch chuckled grimly. 'I doubt it. I left him with wounds he won't get through licking for a month! I'll have a buddy of mine at the camp call you in the evenings for a while, but I think you'll be safe enough. Just keep your doors locked and don't open them to anyone—'cept me, that is.' And, grinning, he took her into his arms.

'Will I—be seeing you then?' she asked, a trifle breathlessly, straining back against the impelling pressure of his arms.

'Probably not until our wedding day,' against her cheek.

'No, Mitch, I told you ...' But his mouth, gliding down her cheek, closed over hers, effectively stopping her protest. His lips moved in gentle but firm insistence until she could no longer resist their drugging effect nor the pressure of his arms. He drew her forward until she felt crushed against his chest, but still, as if mindful of her ordeal the night before, he refrained from using force on her mouth, coaxing her lips to part and respond to his with just a measure of the abundant expertise at his disposal.

When eventually he lifted his head, he stood loosening his hold on her and looking into her upturned face with an indecipherable half-smile on his. 'You think about it and I'm certain your answer will be yes. Because, my blonde slit-eyed little witch, you want me just as much as I want you.'

Gina stiffened, both excited at the throbbing quality of his voice and yet repelled at what he said, and tried to free herself from the suddenly ineluctable barrier of his arms. 'I am not slit-eyed!' she objected. 'And neither am I panting to go to bed with you. Now let me go!'

'Little liar!' he jeered. 'And while you're certainly not slit-eyed now, you weren't standing where I was just a moment ago.'

'You! You're insufferable!' she told him, striking at his upper arms with her fists. But she might just as well have beat them against the trunk of a giant oak. 'Let me *go!*'

'Okay—for the time being.' Mitch dropped a kiss on the corner of her mouth. *'Aloha oe.'* And he was gone.

CHAPTER EIGHT

GINA sat back in her seat and tried to relax, to sleep. But in vain. To relax was impossible and sleep itself was as far removed from her as was the Pacific Ocean that lay below the body of the Boeing 747 jet. Not that the ocean could be seen through the small double-glazed window situated alongside her. There was nothing but pitch blackness. They had been flying eight hours and there was still another eight hours stretching mercilessly ahead of her in which to further meditate upon her folly.

She looked down at her left hand and stared at the gold band on her third finger, still bright, new and unfamiliar. Mitch had been right. She had said yes and the wedding had been a quiet affair, the ceremony performed in the garden of her parents' home under the auspices of their local pastor. Their wedding night, and the only one available to them before Mitch's return flight to Honolulu, had been spent in their parents' double guest room. Her parents had tactfully suggested that they might like to spend their first night alone somewhere over on the nearby coast, but Mitch had discounted this idea, much to Gina's increased agitation.

'I can't sleep with you here, under my parents' roof,' she had told him baldly when they were alone in their room. 'I just can't!'

'I know it,' had been his astonishing reply.

'Then—then why didn't you follow up my parents' suggestion?'

'And go over to the coast?' He had come forward and taken her gently in his arms. 'Because tomorrow I have to leave you. I don't want to arrive back on Oahu after one night with you, the memory of which will only serve to tear my insides out night after night until you're able to join me. Besides, you're wound up and as taut as a harp string,' he added, lowering his head to press a brief kiss into the hollowed curve between her neck and shoulder. 'When we first make love,' he continued, looking into her face, 'I want nothing on your mind except me. No thought of parents, or of our imminent separation, or worries about leasing your house and giving up your job. I want you used to me and trusting me—and wanting me to the exclusion of everything else.' He had moved away from her and had began to undress, while Gina had remained quite still, her eyes staring darkly, more grey than green, out of her pale face. She had spoken through stiff lips:

'What if I don't come? What if once you've gone, I change my mind?'

'That possibility had crossed my mind,' Mitch had owned, unbuttoning his shirt. 'But that's a risk it's necessary I take. However, I think you're the kind of person who, once she has made her bed, will lie on it . . .'

The conversation had taken place between them at the beginning of April. It was now the end of June. Mitch's letters to her during this period of separation had been frequent and interesting, betraying no sentiment or expressing any heartfelt wish that she was there beside him. It seemed obvious to her that he was giving her plenty of opportunity to think and to change her mind if she wished. The marriage had not been consummated and so an annulment would not be difficult to obtain.

But although she was tempted many times to rescind her resignation at work, and to cancel the newspaper advertisement which enumerated the attractive features of her house to prospective lessees, several unvarying factors always prevented her. No one at work had known of her marriage. This was a safeguard she had taken in the event that upon further deliberation she should decide to have the marriage annulled. But what would have happened to her if she had so chosen and opted to remain in her job where her only enjoyment was in the carrying out of her work? And to go on living in her attractive little house, safe and secure, for the rest of her life, positive that there would be no more brash, sanguine strangers disrupting her life? Would the hobbies she had so enjoyed and the ambitions that had sustained her for so long continue to do so when she knew with absolute certainty that the memory of the time she had been needed would never leave her?

Mitch had outlined all the practical reasons why they should marry and had admitted to desiring her, but of the fact that he needed her, quite desperately, he had made no mention. That he desired her, she found acceptable, for she too desired him in return. It was a mystery to her that she should; especially since at the beginning, and even well on in their acquaintance, she had found him totally objectionable, but it was one into which she didn't care to delve too deeply. He didn't love her, but that did not concern her. Rather to the contrary. The fact that neither was in love with the other was in itself a blessing, a safeguard. Love was a mighty force, a powerful weapon that when in the wrong hands, wielded the wrong way, could destroy, or at least do irreparable damage. She never wished to court another such tragedy, nor be in possession of the power to inflict such pain on another. What had finally been the deciding factor behind the acceptance of Mitch's proposal had been that he needed her. He had never once said so, but she was as instinctively sure of this as she was of her own name.

And in her surfaced a corresponding desire to be needed, one which, on having to realise that Norrie didn't need her and never had and never would, she had spent a long time and had been relentless in subjugating. Nobody had ever needed her, neither at work nor within the gardens and four empty walls of her house. And while she had once found this an entirely satisfactory situation to be in, she knew now that to pick up the threads of such a life would utterly destroy her. To be needed by Mitch and possibly a small motherless little girl was a project into which she considered it worth investing her life. The odds were that if she retreated she might never be needed again. In return for her investment, her own need to be needed would be met, and Mitch, she knew without a qualm, would prove himself as a man of integrity and would respect and be true to her. What more could one ask out of life? There were many who were offered, and had to be satisfied with a great deal less.

By the time she had arrived at Honolulu airport, early morning Hawaiian time, Gina was gritty-eyed and exhausted. The mirror in the aircraft's toilet cubicle was less than kind, reflecting lank hair, inflamed eyes and a skin that both looked and felt as pale and dry as paper. Was this to be Mitch's first glimpse of her? If only she could have slept or at least have had, in lieu of sleep, a bath and a change of clothing.

Upon clearing Customs, she made the discovery that she was to have her wish, and it turned out to be accompanied by such an unpalatable condition she wanted only to revoke it.

'Where's Mitch?' she asked Lou de Laney, immediately on the defensive, not bothering to return his greeting which, on the surface, had been cordial enough, but Gina didn't need keen percipience to sense in him the undercurrent of hostility which was swift to strike an answering spark within herself.

'Mitch has been unavoidably detained,' he drawled. 'It's an occurrence you'll have to get used to, being married to a soldier, so now's as good a time as any to start getting used to the life. Shall we go fetch your luggage?'

All of a sudden, Gina felt as though she had made the unwisest move of her life. A tide of homesickness swept over her and carried her precariously close to tears. She forcibly swallowed back the salt lump that had risen to her throat and followed behind Lou, endeavouring to appear as dignified and composed as she could.

'Is this all?' asked Lou, looking down in surprise at her two medium-sized suitcases.

'Yes. I was over the weight allowance as it was.'

'You don't envisage this marriage being a long-term affair, then?'

Gina's eyes conveyed her dislike of him and they burned with the intensity of it.

'There's not one facet of our marriage that has anything to do with you,' she stated emphatically, and although she was aware of herself entering into a state of ague, she managed to keep her voice steady and evenly pitched.

'The hell there isn't!' came his grim retort, and lifting the two suitcases, he left her to make her own way behind him through the crowd of meandering strangers.

They drove in silence and Gina utilised the time spent seated beside him in the two-door Mustang to observe the paradise isle which was to be her home. Even away from the airport, where everyone except herself had been greeted with leis of colourful carnations, white gardenias or waxlike frangipani, the hot air was sweet with perfume and heavy with moisture. Up until the car had been set in motion it had felt almost too thick to breathe.

Gina didn't know what she expected Honolulu to look like. She knew that she, presumably like everyone else who had never visited the islands, had an idyllic picture that automatically rose before the mind's eye whenever the name Hawaii was mentioned. But now, faced with the reality, she found it impossible to conjure up her original concept. All she could be sure of was that it had contained no criss-crossing network of well travelled freeways, or great conglomerations of power poles and power lines, or vast areas of tightly packed skyscrapers or innumerable apartment blocks and dingy little bungalows which, once away from Honolulu, spread ever onward mile after mile over an undulating terrain that, at first glance at least, appeared stark and treeless. The mountains, which to Gina represented the only welcome sight, rose in the distance almost sheer, very rugged and certainly majestic, clothed royally in lush emerald foliage.

After about a twenty-five-minute drive, Lou pulled off the freeway and eventually slowed and drew to a halt outside a low bungalow situated on a corner section. It was dull green in colour with a matching picket fence, screened doors and windows and set amid tropical plants, the hibiscus, banana and ginger plants being the only ones among them that Gina was able to put names to.

As she gazed upon her new home, her heart sank and she was grateful that Lou's sapient gaze was able only to see the back of her head. With what she hoped he would have to interpret as alacrity, she gathered up her hand luggage and struggling up out of the low-slung car, preceded him up the broken path which was flanked on either side by two small areas of rather coarse-looking grass. The interior of the bungalow, she was grateful to discover, was a vast improvement on the exterior, spacious and uncluttered, the paintwork, wallpaper, curtains and all other fittings and furniture being in surprisingly good condition.

'It's lovely,' she breathed, going from one room to the next, and yet while the décor wasn't strictly to her taste, she knew there was no faulting it.

'Isn't it though?' Lou agreed dryly. 'I thought it was just as good the way it was before, but Mitch was determined to redecorate the place before the arrival of his bride.'

'Then I must remember to tell him how much I appreciate it,' Gina returned equably. 'I like it very much indeed. And it seems so much cooler in here.'

'Mitch left the air-conditioning on this morning—to ensure that you'd be comfortable.'

With an effort, Gina kept her head lifted high and her manner and expression unruffled. 'When will Mitch be home, do you know?'

'No, but compared to the attractions which now await him at home, there'll be nothing to keep him at the post, will there?'

'And you resent that, don't you?'

His eyes narrowed and his fists clenched as he took a step towards her, appearing so full of malevolence that Gina had to steel herself from retreating from him. 'What I resent,' he said as through gritted teeth, 'is not that he should be hooked, but that he should be hooked by the likes of someone as unworthy as you.'

Ineffably weary, Gina passed a hand across her eyes, saying: 'Look, I know you don't like me, that there's no love lost between either of us, but do we have to go on tearing at each other like this? It seems so senseless.'

'There's no love in you for anyone, not just me. No one, not even Mitch.'

Gina stared at the angry young man confronting her in a tired, helpless silence.

'Is there? Can you honestly stand there and tell me you married Mitch because you love him?'

She gestured with her hands, trying to explain: 'You don't understand, Lou. We didn't marry because we'd fallen madly in love with each other. Either of us . . .'

Lou swore, awe mingling with the frustration in his

voice. 'You sure take the cake! Why else would Mitch surrender the freedom he's cherished for so long? On a whim? Or so as to provide some poor unfortunate kid with a mother? Or simply in order to get you into his bed?' He laughed harshly. 'As screwed up as you are, he'd never have had to marry you to get you into his bed!'

White and drained, both physically and emotionally, Gina pointed towards the door. 'Please go. Just go!'

Her voice was hollow and lacking in impetus, but he must have recognised that she was at the end of her tether, for he made to leave, turning back before passing through the doorway. 'I'll leave, only too glad to, but, sister, I'm warning you, if you betray Mitch's love for you, I swear I'll swing for you!' And he slammed the door shut after him.

'Welcome to Paradise!' Gina uttered aloud, and went into the bedroom, dropping her handbag on to the kingsize double bed and crossing to stare out of the bedroom window at the countless other bungalows dotted like boxes across the slopes of the hills which spread before her. As the aircraft had come in to land, she had seen a port and harbour which could have been a port or harbour anywhere in the world, but nowhere had she caught a glimpse of a beach, and even though she went to investigate the view from every window in the house, there was still not a beach to be seen.

After showering, washing and drying her hair and changing into a cotton knit nightdress which fell loosely over her body, supported by two narrow shoulder straps, she pulled the curtains and slipped wearily in between the sheets on the vast bed and lay measuring the space she had with outstretched arms. It could fit four people and there would still be room to spare. And she remembered her incredulous amazement as she had left the airport building to be immediately greeted by the sight of numerous parked, six-door limousines. She had opened her mouth to give voice to her first impression that the cars needed an extra set of wheels, but on glimpsing Lou's formidable expression she had quickly closed it again. She and Lou would never be friends. He had in his mind a picture of her just the same as she had had in her mind a picture of Honolulu.

Reality painted quite a different picture altogether. And since she was under the misconception that Mitch was in love with her while she, the siren he fancied her to be, was prepared only to receive it and never give it, it was only to be expected that he should feel such concern for his friend's emotional welfare. When the opportunity presented itself she would have to put it to Mitch that he set the younger man's mind at rest or else the tension that would doubtless arise in the event of their inevitable meetings would be intolerable.

It was late afternoon when she awoke and her sleep had been so deep and sound it took some time to adjust her thoughts and remember where she actually was. Groggily, she climbed out of bed and padded into the bathroom, where she brushed her teeth and rinsed her face over and over with cold water until she felt more alert. She dried herself, soothed moisturiser into her parched skin, brushed her hair and then, somewhat diffidently, made her way to the lounge.

It was bathed in shadows and there was not a sound. Then, as she was about to proceed further, her wandering gaze fell on the still silent form of Mitch stretching out on the couch, and she realised that this was the first time she had seen him in his uniform. She crossed over quietly and knelt on the rug beside the couch and was glad of the opportunity, however brief, which would allow her to study him unawares.

When he did awake he was not like she had been. His eyes opened and instantly he was wide awake, staring into her face with his comprehending powers unimpaired by the effects of sleep. His hand reached out to touch her hair. 'How long have you been there?'

Gina smiled, inclining the side of her face against his palm. 'Not long. I just wanted to see if you'd changed at all—before I wakened you.'

'And how would you have wakened me?' he murmured, and his eyes, smiling slumbrously, roamed her face before moving down over her neck and bare shoulders and peaked breasts provocatively concealed by the skimpy cotton knit nightdress. Sliding off the couch to join her on the rug, he pulled her down with him until she lay against him, clasped tightly in his arms. She found herself being kissed without preliminaries, but was made to feel, as she responded with a hunger as raw as his own, that preliminaries didn't matter and might never matter again.

Without lifting his mouth from hers, he moved her until she was sandwiched between the hard rug-covered floor and the length of his body, and although her senses revelled in the strength and weight of him, she was finally forced to whimper: 'You're squashing me!'

Eventually her message penetrated through to him, and with a sigh and a mumbled apology, he ceased his exploration of the side of her neck, which it had delighted her to expose to him, and shifted to lie propped up on one elbow beside her.

'Are we doomed to always make love on the floor?' she asked with a smile she found difficult to maintain. 'Your floor's a lot harder than mine!'

His eyes were so intent on their exploration of her face, she wondered if he even heard, much less comprehended what she had said.

'I've missed you.' The throbbing quality of his voice found its echo somewhere deep within her, causing her to tremble with the intensity of her desire for him. As he leaned to press his lips into the pulsating hollow of her throat, Gina lifted her hands to hold his head. Fingers curled into his hair and tightened as his lips trailed downwards and the hand which had been rhythmically moulding and pressing her abdomen slid up to encircle her breast. His thumb and lips brushed alternately over the tip causing his name to burst from her lips on a gasp.

All of a sudden he wrenched himself away from her and hauled himself to his feet. 'I'm sorry,' he said huskily, reaching down for both her hands and drawing her up on to her feet. 'I'm behaving like a selfish swine.' With his arms linked loosely about her he kissed her forehead. 'If you slept all day you must be ravenous. Before I nodded off, I thought of a little restaurant down on Waikiki beach. It's intimate, cosy and has great atmosphere. I'll ring and make a reservation for around eight. How's that? One and a half hours should be enough time to get ready, shouldn't it?'

As he spoke, Gina gazed at him in mute stupefaction. Darkness was falling extraordinarily quickly and she knew that he would be unable to read her expression nor did he seen able to sense her keen disappointment.

'How do you like the house?' he asked, leaving her side to switch on the lamp resting on a table beside the couch. 'Or perhaps it's too soon for you to make up your mind? Did Lou show you over it when your arrived?'

Gina nodded and, moistening her lips with the tip of her tongue, tried desperately to get her thoughts assembled in some kind of order.

'The second bedroom—is it for Kim-Lan? It's delightfully decorated for a little girl.'

'What about the first bedroom?' Mitch laughed, obviously experiencing no inclination to let Kim-Lan be introduced into the conversation. 'I hope it's just as delightfully decorated for a big girl.'

'I've never had an en-suite before. It's lovely, Mitch, it really is,' she replied with all the enthusiasm she could muster, while everything in her rebelled at having to carry on this, what seemed to her at a time like this, inane conversation.

She sat before her dressing-table mirror and listened as if in a daze to Mitch humming to himself as he showered. Her hand clutched about the handle of her brush while eyes, glazed and misted, started back at her from the mirror. How could he? She thrust the brush into her lap. How could be be so insensitive? Every fibre of her being was crying out for fulfilment, every emotion tense, waiting expectantly for a release that Mitch seemed to want to provide one minute and yet able the next to appear as though his ardour was as swift to die as it was to rise. Food! The very thought was enough to choke her . . .

At that point Mitch, still humming off-key, returned to their room, a towel about his waist while with

another he was drying his hair. He stopped suddenly as
though becoming aware of the unconscious intensity of
her gaze on him. He looked over at her and their eyes
met in the mirror. 'You haven't even begun to get
ready . . . Is something the matter?'

She shook her head. 'I'm—I'm not really hungry,
Mitch.'

He came to stand behind her, placing his hands on
her shoulders, gently massaging the back of her neck
with his thumbs. 'What is it?' he asked with concern.
'Are you feeling homesick already?'

Despairing, Gina lowered her eyes, and her head, in
obedience to a will of its own, replied in the negative
and then leaned back against the tautly defined muscles
of his stomach. She heard the sharp intake of his
breath, felt him stir.

'Look at me, Gina,' he ordered softly, and with
eyelids heavy with reluctance to concur she finally lifted
to the mirror to meet his.

'Are you seducing me?' he asked, still in the same
tone of voice.

'No, I am not!' she snapped and, stiffening instantly,
made to jerk away from him, but his hands resisted her
attempts to escape and forced her back until contact
with him was restored with more intimacy than she
herself would have ever dreamed of establishing. 'It
was you who began the seduction scene,' she pointed
out frigidly, 'not me.'

For a short period his gaze continued to hold her
proud defiant one which was no longer glazed with
emotion but instead frosted with disdain. 'I'm sorry,' he
apologised at last. 'I thought I was doing you a
favour—I thought you needed time to get used to me
again. At least that's what I've spent these past months
telling myself I would have to allow for. It seems that
I've programmed myself so successfully, I failed to
recognise a response that would negate it . . .'

'It doesn't matter,' Gina mumbled, so embarrassed
now she wanted only to escape him and the four walls
of the room that were slowly but surely closing in on
her. 'Let's go and eat.'

But still he resisted her efforts to disengage herself. Indignantly, she glared at him, in the face of which he smiled slowly. And just as slowly, he drew aside her hair, lowered his head and pressed his mouth to the curve of her neck and shoulder while sliding his hands down over the soft roundness of her arms.

Determined to hang on to the remaining shreds of her pride, she maintained her posture of rigidity. 'How long does it take to drive to Waikiki?' she asked pointedly.

'To hell with Waikiki!' he said harshly. 'And don't adopt that tone with me, you little cat! I've waited for you a damn sight longer than you've waited for me, I can tell you!' And in a manner that tolerated no further argument or resistance, he slid the straps of her nightdress over her shoulders and watched with eyes suddenly as dark as ink, as the material slithered down over her breasts to fall in folds about her hips.

With a sighing intake of breath, he drew her to her feet and turned her around. Gina watched him, mesmerised, and his eyes gazed back at her lazily mocking as he said, his hands following the descent of the cotton over her hips: 'I think this augurs very well for our future.'

Positive he was gloating, she wanted suddenly to hit out at him with both fists, but as his lips came down to claim hers and her breasts were crushed against his chest, her fingers unfurled and of their own accord, slid up and clutched at his neck. The sudden spasming of his arms around her and the unexpected hardening of his mouth on hers evoked a response within her so acute she was rendered dazed and helpless, and thoughts and senses merged, falling prey to passion. Delighting in the feel of his mouth, she quivered as lips explored the satin-smooth planes of her face, the curves beneath her brows, her ears and the more sensitive areas of her neck. Then, as if independently aware of her expanding need to be even closer to him than she was, her hands lowered to close over the bunches of the towel about his waist, tugging at the only barrier left between them.

'Pull it off, don't play with it!' Mitch ordered against her mouth in a voice as rasping as his breath.

She did so slowly yet with an inexplicable sense of authority that was, at the same time, both old and new, as though it had always resided within her, latent and unclaimed. Dropping her flushed face in order to press kisses against the hard column of his throat, across his collarbone and lower to where the deep concave extended down the centre of his chest, she revelled in this opportunity to taste, smell and her fingers to feel as, once having accomplished their task, they splayed to caress his ribcage before moving to find new delight in the feel under them the skin of his muscular back.

'Not so fastidious now, are you, my little surprise packet?' came his uneven taunt as a single painful tug on her hair tipped her face, exposing it to his merciless scrutiny. But if his wish was to intimidate her, he failed, for as he gathered her to him, her breath caught and she gave herself up to her first experience of what it was to feel a body, warm, bare and vital, against the length of her own. Lost, she subsided against him and heard his smothered exclamation as his hands dropped to her hips to lock her to him.

Her gaze fever-bright and heavy-lidded, she stared back at him, knowing that she should be the first one to be surprised and shocked at her own actions, but she had been made too drunk by the overriding intoxication of her own discoveries to care what he thought or to consider the propriety of her behaviour. Instead, she entwined her fingers in his hair and brought his face down to hers, compelling him to kiss her, harder, more urgently, until awareness of all else receded.

When later it returned it was to find herself lying with Mitch looming over her, the soft light from her dressing table glancing off his shoulders. 'The light,' she whispered, her breath constricting suddenly as his fingers wended a sensuous trail from her breasts to her abdomen, startling shivers all through her.

'You're not going to try now to convince me you're shy?' he challenged with velvet-clad scorn.

But as his mouth embarked upon the same path as his fingers, there was no desire in her to answer . . .

When she awoke it was still dark. She frowned. She couldn't remember it having been this dark, for the last thing she recalled . . . abruptly, she twisted around and sighting Mitch's sleeping head on the pillow beside hers, relaxed with a sigh and uncurled and stretched languorously . . . she was cleaving and crying out to him, and then his damp face was buried in the curve of her neck. It must have been he who had switched off the dressing table lamp after she had been swept into an oblivion as soft and as luxurious as mink.

As the dawn light stole softly into the room, she rolled on to her stomach and lay observing the man who was her husband. Somehow, the act of waking up to find this man in bed beside her seemed to be one of even greater intimacy than all that had gone before it. Then it had seemed so right, so utterly inevitable, as though predestined from the beginning of time. In the cold light of morning, however, she felt something akin to dismay. They had come together like animals, she thought, and for the first time she could begin to consider the moral aspect of making love with a man she didn't love, whether in or outside the bonds of matrimony. And while it hadn't been an issue the night before, belated shadows of guilt and shame now sidled in, causing her to bite down troubledly on her lip. She had agreed to this marriage because she knew that if neither was in love with the other, neither could hurt the other, and she had subsequently found that what she had suspected of herself was true. She could give herself more abandonedly to this man than she could ever have done at twenty-two had she married Norrie, for her lack of love for Mitch set her free from inhibitions plus constant worry of what he might think of how she might appear to him. As things stood between them it was simply of no consequence. However, she had never bargained on there being any after-effects such as shame or guilt . . .

With his usual disconcerting swiftness, Mitch awoke to find her eyes upon him. He smiled at her sleepily and stretched with unselfconscious ease. 'Gina, Gina,' he murmured, reaching his hand out to rest its palm against the side of her face, bringing the ball of his thumb across her parted lips. 'Mine at last. And always had been—who would have thought?'

And over the days that followed, he often teased her about her virgin condition. And because this embarrassed her intensely, she decided that the delight he was afforded by this discovery was a trifle exorbitant, to say the least. Still, there was not much she could do other than ignore his teasing and try not to let it, as well as the gentle, almost loving attitude which accompanied and even extended beyond it, affect her to too great an extent.   The morning immediately following her arrival in Honolulu they left by air for the island of Maui on which, she discovered, Mitch owned a condominium situated approximately twenty minutes by car from the quaint old village of Lahaina. It was one of several situated on a prime site only a matter of five seconds' walk from the beach. The money Mitch had used to purchase the compact self-contained unit had been that left to him by his uncle. It hadn't been much, but then in those days, property on Maui hadn't been as inordinately expensive as it was today. To buy a condominium on Maui would prove a sound investment, he had been assured by a friend whom he trusted and whose judgement he respected. His friend had been right. The amount now being offered for the property, a modest one by Gina's own standards, was so enormous she found herself incapable of assimilating it no matter how hard she tried.

From their second-story patio, they had an uninterrupted view of the golf course, dotted with palms that swayed in a gentle but persistent breeze, the blue Pacific etched against the horizon in one direction and lush green cloud-piercing mountains against the other, but no matter how much time she spent contemplating, Gina never came any closer to comprehending the stories, similar to this one, that were related to her. Finally, because the tales she was hearing were beginning to depress her, she had to plead with Mitch to stop. The exotic beauty of the island was being spoilt for her. She enjoyed their sunrise excursion to the crater of the ten-thousand-foot dormant volcano, Haleakala, their extensive trips taken over unsealed volcanic roads, past sugar cane plantations and through mountainous rain forests, and their frequent visits to the attractive village of Lahaina where many of the shops were built on stilts and extended out over the water. On the face of it, evidence of man's greed and exploitation of the island wasn't visible, and she didn't want to be made morbid by Mitch's revealing to her the corruption that seethed behind the tranquil, awe-inspiring beauty.

Mitch had sighed and had acquiesced. Part of the reason why she couldn't cope with such sordid revelations was due to the country she came from, he told her. Unspoilt, unexploited and underpopulated, with beaches and beauty that would far surpass all she saw here and yet were within the reach of all, not only those who could afford it. Could you blame persons such as these, he asked, who lived all their lives in concrete jungles with their feet cushioned by nothing softer than bitumen, endless bitumen, wanting to stake their claim in a place they could look upon as Paradise?

Paradise! Before too many weeks had passed, Gina had drawn her own private conclusion that she was living anywhere but in Paradise.

Mitch had shown her almost all there was to see on the island of Oahu and at the end of each expedition would sit back and wait, silently, watchfully, for her reaction. She had soon grown wise to his tactics, and adopted for herself a deliberately blasé attitude, and she knew to brace herself afresh each day for further exposure to the unpredictability of his nature. One day he would drive her through the élite suburbs where, in quiet palm-lined avenues, behind the splendour of tropical fauna, lay the secluded homes of the wealthy, spectacular homes such as she had never seen before. Then, as if to blot this picture totally from her mind, he would drive his Chevrolet convertible through slums which evoked a dazed silence from quite a separate source.

Waikiki, situated on one side of the island, was a hive of tourist industry, a picture of wealth and prosperity. Banks, hotels, and office blocks covered every inch of Kalakaua Avenue which, for the most part, lay parallel with the famous beach. On the opposite side of the island, another altogether different scene greeted her, and a sensation that she had stepped back several decades descended upon her. To Gina, there was no evidence anywhere of tender concern shown by speculators in the way the land had been carved and bulldozed to make way for new housing, new developments, new projects. It had been a brutal and greedy hand that had taken and moulded the island.

The contrasts seemed never-ending. Downtown Honolulu and the infamous Chinatown were the next two sights listed on Mitch's private itinerary, and as he drew to a halt in Beach Street, he turned off the ignition and lounged back in his seat, spreading both arms, draping one along the back of their seats and the other along the door.

Gina looked sideways at him and seconds later suddenly broke down and found herself laughing as though she'd never be able to stop.

'What's up?' he asked as she sat back in her seat, sobering and shaking her head.

'Oh, no,' she was quick to reprove him. 'That is precisely *my* question. Why all these plunges into paradise one day, out and into hell the next? I barely finish catching my breath in awe and it's promptly turned into a gasp of horror!'

'I just wanted you to get a balanced view of your future home.'

Gina gazed at him, and all at once, for a reason that totally eluded her, she was swamped in an onrush of tenderness. And, laughingly caught up into this strange new emotion for him, she reached over, took his face in her hands and kissed him with more sweetness than she had ever shown him. When she drew back, it was to find he hadn't moved a muscle. His eyes, fixed on hers, had an arrested look, while at the same time they had darkened with a disturbing intensity. She released him quickly and looked away, wondering at herself. She had never been the one to volunteer any demonstration of affection before and when he had done so to her, she had told herself it was because he was a demonstrative person, as Americans on the whole tended to be, and with this conclusion and generalisation arrived at and blithely accepted, she had pondered no further. Perhaps the trait was contagious, she thought, gazing about her at the shabby somnolent street, which appeared innocuous and, to her mind, somehow disappointing in the brilliant sunlight.

'It doesn't look particularly dangerous,' she shrugged, and gave a sharp cry of pain as Mitch's hand flashed out, caught her face in suddenly brutal fingers and jerked it around until her widened eyes were able to see the gravity in his.

'I don't care how country-townish this may look to you,' he said grimly. 'I've told you you're never to come here alone, either day or night, and I want to know right now that you understand what I'm saying!'

'Mitch! You're hurting me!'

'Do you understand' he asked, his grip tightening relentlessly.

'*Yes!*'

A second or two later, he seemed satisfied enough to set her free.

'Was that display of brute strength really necessary?' Gina demanded, rubbing the sides of her face with both hands.

'That was a caress compared to what I'll do to you if I ever find out you've disobeyed me, Gina.'

'Honestly, Mitch! You're sounding positively mid-Victorian!'

He sighed impatiently, starting the car. 'I know you're a small town girl . . .'

Gina's head rounded in indignation. 'I'll have you know that by our standards, Palmerston is a city!'

'. . . . but even so,' he continued as though she hadn't spoken, 'surely even you can understand the seriousness of those crimes reported in the news bulletins?'

The reports of the crime committed on the island

broadcast at intervals over the radio had taken Gina a long time to get used to. Some of the cases reported were so grisly, so mind-boggling, that she had had to find comfort somehow, so she had begun switching off the radio, consoling herself with her conviction that they were as exaggerated as everything else on the island.

'Mitch! Mitch!' At the sound of the high-pitched accented voice calling so excitedly, Mitch allowed the car to stall and turned to see who it was hailing him. A tall long-haired Chinese girl was running along the pavement as fast as her backless high-heeled shoes and narrow slitted skirt would allow. She reached Mitch's side of the car panting decorously, her lovely Oriental features lit up by her smile. A long-fingered, scarlet-tipped hand, the the colour of pale ivory, came to rest along his face and full scarlet lips lowered to press a kiss on his cheek. 'It's so good to see you, Mitch. Long time no see. Where've you been?'

'Hi, Mi-Ling.' He took her hand and before Gina's astonished eyes he pressed a kiss on to her knuckles and continued holding her hand while he talked with her, asking her how life was and mentioning names of people he had never spoken to her about.

'But enough of me,' Mi-Ling cast a sly look at Gina. 'Why have I not seen you in such a long time?'

'I've got myself married.' He turned to Gina and to her utter amazement his face took on a sheepish hue as Mi-Ling shrieked with delighted laughter.

'Oh, no!' she trilled in her exquisite voice. 'Not you, Mitch!'

'It's not that funny,' Mitch growled.

'Caught at last! And who landed the biggest fish in all Hawaii?'

Obligingly, Mitch introduced the two women.

'I am pleased to meet you, Gina.' Mi-Ling smiled with genuine pleasure. 'What a man you have! I envy you. Ah, Mitch,' she returned her attention to this man who was suddenly a stranger to Gina. Mi-Ling looked upon him, a faraway, almost melancholy expression in her almond-shaped eyes, while her red-tipped fingers picked up and dropped strands of his hair. She bent suddenly and whispered something into his ear. To Gina's further astonishment she saw a tinge of red steal under Mitch's tan and he threw back his head and laughed.

'*Ciao.*' The girl's smile and wave embraced them both as she turned and, with her hips swaying with unconscious grace, walked away.

On the drive home Mitch didn't speak of the girl, at whose age Gina couldn't even hazard a guess, nor did he disclose what she had said in parting. The effort it cost Gina to refrain from asking was considerable. They arrived home and without waiting for him to open the door for her, she climbed out of the car and resisted the urge to slam the door closed after her.

'What's the big hurry?' asked Mitch, catching up with her half way along the path.

'We've been invited to Carol and Larry's for dinner, remember,' Gina replied as lightly as she could. 'At the rate we're going we'll be late!'

CHAPTER NINE

CAROL and Larry Hutchins with their two children, Ben aged ten and Amanda aged eight, were friends of Mitch's and had very quickly extended their friendship to incorporate Gina as well.

As a rule, after their parting, Gina was left feeling as though she could have quite happily remained in their company for several hours longer. They were so natural and such a happy family. But not this particular night, however. She arrived back home with Mitch feeling strangely enervated and emotionally drained and yet at the same time too mentally active to even contemplate sleep.

Relieved when Mitch kissed her goodnight, having accepted without question her desire to stay up to fix herself a drink and read for a while, she went through the motions of preparing a hot drink with the vague hope that it would relax her.

It had been quite an end to a day that had began in the way they usually began one of Mitch's days off. First had come their encounter with the mysterious Mi-Ling. And between that and their departure for Carol and Larry's they had received news that Kim-Lan would be arriving on a flight from Bangkok on Saturday morning. That was the extent of the information outlined in the Immigration Authorities' telegram, leaving it up to Mitch to contact them for further details.

Gina took her mug of steaming chocolate-coloured liquid into the dining-room and sat down at the table. She placed the mug on a cork-inlaid coaster, rested her face in her hands, and recalled word for word the conversation which had taken place between her and Carol during the time they had been alone together in the kitchen.

'You're very quiet this evening, Gina,' Carol had remarked lightly. 'Nothing wrong, is there?'

'Oh, no.' Unaware that she had been unduly quiet, Gina decided that she had better make a conscious effect to rally and exert herself. 'It's just that I've seen so much today and I realise now I've forgotten to ask Mitch many questions. I wonder how the native Hawaiians feel about their prime land being taken over the way it has.'

Carol sighed. 'Unfortunately, that's something that's happened everywhere—at least I would imagine it has, even in your country, I expect.'

Gina found to her surprise she had to admit that it had. Again, she lapsed into silent.

'Honey,' Carol prodded again, obviously concerned, 'you're not regretting that Mitch is adopting this little Vietnamese girl, are you?'

Gina looked up aghast. 'Oh no! Not at all.' Then she gestured helplessly. How could she explain to Carol, who was in love with a man who loved her in return, that she was married to a man who told her nothing? What she knew about his boyhood she had learned when he had been caught in a weak unguarded moment—a lapse that hadn't been repeated since. Apart from that, what she knew about Mitch and all that went into making up his past life amounted to nothing. She knew he professed to be one who considered the past to be past, but even so, she knew without a shadow of a doubt that all that had taken place in his past was affecting him still, and very deeply, if not in his waking hours then most definitely in his sleeping ones. If only she could help him ... 'What makes you think I would regret it?' she asked, aware suddenly that she had become introspective again and that Carol was watching her.

'As I said, you've been very quiet this evening. What have you been thinking about?'

'About Kim-Lan, I suppose. I only hope I can cope with what's expected of me. Even just to *know* what's expected of me would be an advantage. I know nothing whatsoever of the kind of life the little girl's coming from.'

'Haven't you asked Mitch?' asked Carol in surprise.

'He doesn't talk about Vietnam,' Gina confessed expressionlessly.

Carol fell silent. 'No,' she sighed after a long time. 'No, I expect he doesn't. Neither is he alone in that. Larry doesn't talk about it either. Not many do.'

Gina wanted to blurt out that all she learned was what Mitch muttered and shouted about in his sleep, but resolutely she held her tongue.

'They went through hell, and that's the truth. They saw horrendous, unforgettable atrocities. They lost their best friends. But none of them saw worse than what Mitch saw. And none of them lost their best friend the way Mitch lost his.'

'Is he—is he buried over there?' asked Gina, thinking quickly and deciding not to withdraw but to flounder on, to stab about in the dark. If she asked all the right questions, all to the good. If her questions betrayed her abysmal ignorance, then that was a risk she had to take.

'Goodness, I don't expect he's buried at all. The Viet-Cong would have gone to the spot where he fell, only to see if he were dead, and they certainly wouldn't have stopped to bury him.'

'Would he—have died in the fall?'

'It's to be hoped and believed so.'

'It's just that he talks about it a lot in his sleep.'

Carol came to her side and put a comforting arm about her shoulders. 'I can't begin to imagine what it must be like to live with a man who has to live with the knowledge that he killed his best friend. Remember that Larry and I know the situation, and both or either of us will always be here any time you want to talk.'

'He keeps—keeps telling him to climb . . .'

Carol's arm tightened about her. 'I know, I know. But he wouldn't—couldn't. He just froze. It was either Eddie or all those men in that helicopter and the rest on the ground. Mitch did what he had to do.'

'But he doesn't see it like that. Obviously he can't.'

'One day, God willing and with you at his side, he'll be able to come to terms with it. Larry was one of those men in that helicopter. He was there and he saw Mitch pluck his best friend off that rope. He knows that had the man in that position, faced with that alternative, been anyone other than Mitch, possibly none of them in the helicopter would have come back. He's quite a man.' Carol hugged her warmly, laughing to relieve the tension.

'So what do I do?' Gina's voice emerged in a whisper, and she wiped furtively at a tear that had won the fight and escaped to slide down her cheek.

'Just love him,' Carol advised gently. 'Love him as much as he loves you. I don't doubt that you do. It's just that you're obviously more conservative in your ways than we are, and the way Mitch's eyes follow your every move presents quite a contrast.'

Had Carol, in her sweet sensitive way, been conveying to Gina that she had guessed the true situation between the two of them? If so, why did she, like Lou, insist that Mitch was in love with her? Gina poked at the skin forming on the surface of her untouched drink with her spoon. He desired her, yes, but love her . . . The idea was ludicrous. Couldn't they recognise the difference? They were simply two compatible animals, living, mating, laughing and enjoying the sun together. And as far as he knew, Mitch had no wish to change or add another dimension to the motivating force behind their compatibility—and neither did she!

With a sigh she rose to her feet, took her drink into the kitchen and tipped it down the sink.

To ensure that she didn't disturb Mitch, she went along to the bathroom that was not adjacent to their bedroom, to wash and brush her teeth. Arriving at the door of their bedroom she was brought to an abrupt standstill by the sight that greeted her. The bedside lamp, that Mitch had no doubt left on for her benefit, spilled its soft glow over the bed, which looked as though it had been slept in unmade for weeks. On top of the rumpled covers, Mitch was writhing and twitching in much the same way as she had seen him do when he had stayed the weekend at Tiraumea, and his arms were flailing spasmodically as they had done that night, about a month ago, when he had wakened her with a blow across the mouth.

Tonight, however, his anguished mumblings had given way to aborted sobs and instead of perspiration, his face was glistening with tears.

With her heart pounding, Gina crept forward and knelt beside the bed. She gazed at him with a compassion that brought her almost to tears herself. Should she waken him? she wondered, racked with fear and indecision. What should she do? Finally she eased herself, fully clothed, on to the bed beside him and began to try to soothe him by caressing him and uttering soft expressions of comfort, until eventually he lay quiet and still with his head against her breast.

She awoke the following morning to find Mitch up, showered and dressed in his beige uniform and seated on the end of the bed in the process of lacing up his shoes.

'Morning,' she greeted him, stretching her limbs, cramped from her not daring to move in the night lest she disturbed him.

He turned his head and grunted in response. 'Is this a new fad, going to bed in your clothes?'

'You were having another nightmare,' said Gina, deciding not to mince words. She propped herself up on one elbow. 'Once I managed to quieten you, I didn't want to risk disturbing you.'

His gaze became even more aloof and he gave another unimpressed grunt. 'Well,' he said, standing up, 'no doubt you'll be happy when Kim-Lan arrives and you can offload your frustrated maternal ministrations on her.'

And with that he was gone, and Gina was left blinking at the spot where he had been. So, he had awoken to find himself being held like a babe against its mother's breast. Slowly she lay back on the bed and staring up at the ceiling, began to wonder dismally if, in marrying Mitch, she had unwittingly bitten off more than she would ever be able to chew.

The minute Gina's eyes alighted on the diminutive figure, so painfully thin, the two bunches of black hair poking out high up from either side of a small face, pale beneath its natural sun-browned colour, and so pathetic and woebegone that Gina's reserve and apprehension melted like a freak fall of snow on a summer's day. Her very heart seemed to dissolve within her in a way she had never experienced before. Love was born there spontaneously for the little scrap of humanity as well as a sense of awe at the privilege that had been granted her. She had been called and placed to love this creature starved of all that most people, in the world she knew, took for granted. She and only she, she thought, crouching before the child, careful not to touch her nor alarm or overwhelm her by giving into her urge to express the emotions which were at that moment dominating her.

For the brief time the child was with them, Gina was aware of nothing or no one else, least of all Mitch, who had, in his turn, been watching her with an expression in his eyes that would have rooted her to the spot had she been confronted by it.

Although she had been examined by the proper medical authorities in Bangkok, Kim-Lan was required to undergo further tests and examinations and so had been hospitalised and separated from them for a further three days preceding her arrival. After which period, Gina knew that the most crucial time of all still lay before them.

As the days passed, she thanked God more and more for the talent children possessed to adapt readily. It did not altogether obviate all problems, but it certainly proved of enormous assistance. Patiently she cared for the child, speaking slowly and clearly even though she knew she understood not a word. She bathed and dressed her gently, slowly, yet with the minimum of fuss, fed her well with fresh meat and vegetables, at the same time ensuring that, while Kim-Lan was given enough on her plate, she remembered that the child was unused to good food—or food at all in any great quantity.

Resolutely quelling all impulses to convey her love by way of physical demonstrations, Gina channelled the force through brief affectionate touches and the warmth of her smiles and glances, determined to bide her time and wait until she had won the child's trust and respect.

While Gina was quick to recognise as days came together to form weeks that it was a difficult time of adjustment for Kim-Lan, she failed to recognise her task as arduous or that Mitch was living a life any less normal than the one he had lived before the child's arrival. Consequently she found herself at a loss to understand his lightning mood changes, his flashes of temper and brooding silences. He seemed not to harbour one ounce of warmth for the child, and the more care and attention she lavished on her, sewing for her, reading to her, taking her on outings, teaching her not to be afraid of the sea and how to enjoy playing in sand and on the swings in the park, the less interest Mitch displayed in the pair of them.

Why? Wasn't she doing what was expected of her? Would it please him more if she were to neglect the responsibility she had agreed to take upon herself when she married him? And who, and where, was the child's father? Surely if Mitch was her natural father, he would want to provide for her out of love—not some obscure sense of duty?

Gina sighed to herself as she wandered without direction through the streets of downtown Honolulu. This was the first period of free time she had had in the two months following Kim-Lan's arrival, and she was secretly relieved to have been able to leave her with Carol to be played with and fussed over by her two children and know that she would not be missed for several hours.

On and on she meandered, relaxing by gradual degrees until her thoughts became as aimless as her steps.

Eventually she came to a corner on which was situated a rather dilapidated shop displaying outside in cardboard boxes: 'New Zealand Apples.' Apples! The sudden realisation struck her that she hadn't seen, much less tasted, a common apple since she had left home. Excitedly, she bought several pounds, her only purchase that day, and as she strolled on, she thought, rather belatedly, to take note of where the shop was located so that she could return. Biting a second time into the yellow and red-skinned flesh, she gazed around her until her eyes located a street sign that made her blood run cold. She was in Hotel Street and had been, it dawned on her, dallying for at least the past three-quarters of an hour in Chinatown.

The sun poured into the near-vacant street which, to Gina's untutored eye, looked for all the world like an old street in one of the older suburbs of the major cities in her own country. Verandahs overhung the pavements, shielding untidy windows which were either filled with junk, books, grocery items, foodstuffs, clothing or covered over with posters. Some were even boarded up. Honestly, she couldn't see what the fuss was about! It was different, interesting, rather like taking a stroll through a shanty town. Besides, she continued on, munching her apple, if it was safe for Mi-Ling to walk here, why shouldn't it be safe for her? However, upon arriving at another corner, she paused and started dubiously up the side street, more narrow, more deserted than the one she was now on. Then with a mental shrug, she adopted an in-for-a-penny-in-for-a-pound attitude and turned to her right.

She was almost at the end of the street when she became aware suddenly that she was no longer a lone walker on the dirty narrow pavement. As she was about to turn casually, her action was intercepted. She was pushed violently from behind and at the same time felt herself jarred as her assailant made a grab for her bag. As she stumbled the apples spilled from her arms and rolled away into the gutter, but she didn't have to worry about her bag, as she had looped the shoulder strap diagonally across her body, not because she had given any thought to thieves, but because it had made it easier for her to manage the bag of apples.

Within her, the functions of her heart and lungs went completely haywire. It took no time at all for her to regain her balance, but as she began to run her legs felt as though they were melting away under her as they did whenever she was caught up in a nightmare that didn't seem any less real than this simply because she happened to be asleep.

She had no idea how much distance she had covered before being caught. She screamed, then sobbed at being forced to accept that the thin powerless shriek she heard was all she had been able to manage. The walls of a dark filthy alley seemed to fall in on her as she was thrust into the dark narrow opening. A stench of rotting garbage filled her nostrils, but mercifully she wasn't called upon to have to suffer it for long. Smells, fear, the ominous lurching of her stomach all ceased, as did her consciousness of everything else as a single savage blow on the side of her head brought a yawning chasm of blackness rushing up to engulf her . . .

How strange to dream that Mitch had been sitting on a chair beside her bed as she lay sleeping, watching her with eyes made more brightly and more intensely blue by tears that shimmered there. She remembered in the dream trying desperately to keep her eyes open to ask him why he was crying, but she couldn't. Still, it had been only a dream, for when she did actually open her eyes, it was to see Mitch prowling about the room.

'Mitch?' Her voice was husky from sleep. 'Why don't you come to bed? Can't you sleep?'

Immediately he was at her side and his eyes, in a shockingly ravaged countenance, were one minute concern-filled, the next blazingly angry. This time Gina wanted only to close her eyes against the sight, but she couldn't. 'Mitch? What's the matter?' Perplexed, she tried to sit up, but was forced to slump back on her pillow as pain, like a sword, drove through her head.

'What's the matter?' he repeated, keeping his voice down, which was obviously calling for tremendous restraint on his part. 'I'll give you "what's the matter"! Didn't I tell you *never* to go to Chinatown on your own? Didn't I explicitly warn you?—didn't I make you listen to and read the news reports? My God, I could wring your fool neck myself! Look at this!' He shoved his hands into his pockets and brought out a narrow length of cream leather and waved the ends of it in front of her stricken eyes. 'Do you recognise this? The strap to your bag, found still over your shoulder. Which meant your attacker was in possession of a knife and not at all averse to using it. The fact that he was satisfied with braining you rather than sticking a knife through your ribs is something I suppose we should be thankful for . . .'

'Mr Mitchell!'

Gina's mind had recovered sufficiently to realise what it was Mitch was angry about and that she was in hospital and the woman who came bustling indignantly into the room was one of the nursing staff.

As Mitch turned to leave without another word, Gina again tried to sit up. Ignoring the pain in her head, she asked plaintively: 'Where are you going?'

From the door he turned and replied with ill-repressed viciousness: 'Somewhere where I can get as drunk as hell!'

Before the nurse had a chance to reprimand him a second time, he had gone.

Speaking soothingly, she encouraged Gina to settle back on the pillow.

'Although it might not appear so, I think it must be his way of expressing his relief that you're on the mend. Your mishap has given him a nasty shock.'

'How—how long have I been here?' Gina asked.

'About three days now.'

Three days! Gina was appalled. 'But,' frantically she caught at the nurse's arm, 'but what about Kim-Lan— my little girl?'

'Now, now, if you want to be out of here as soon as possible, you'll have to stop worrying. Your daughter will be well taken care of, you can be sure of that.'

But Gina knew she wouldn't rest easy until she knew for sure where Kim-Lan was and who was taking care of her.

The moment Mitch appeared the following afternoon and rather strained greetings were exchanged, she asked about Kim-Lan immediately.

Before answering, Mitch walked to the window and stood there for a moment or two in silence, his hands thrust in the pockets of his trousers, pulling the material tautly across his hips. 'Kim-Lan is fine. Carol and Larry volunteered to take care of her until you're fit and well again.'

'You're—you're sure she's all right?' Gina pleaded, tears causing her voice to break.

Mitch returned to her bedside, sat down and stared at her with eyes that were blank in his sombre face. 'She's fine.'

'I've only just managed to get her feeling secure,' Gina explained tearfully. 'I'm sure this will be a terrible setback for her.'

'Children are remarkably resilient, as she's already proved. She'll recover.'

Gina shook her head, grieved by the stony staccato quality of his response. 'Don't you care about her, Mitch?'

'Of course I damn well care about her!' he exploded. 'Why do you think I wanted to adopt her?'

Stung by the anger and exasperation in his response,

she rallied swiftly and responded, her voice stiff and controlled: 'Well, I don't know whether deep down you really do care for her, but I do. I don't know what I'd do if anything happened to her. She's all I've got in the world to love, and I'll love her for you and in spite of you!'

'Yeah,' Mitch sighed quietly, almost wearily. He leaned forward with his elbows resting on his thighs and stared down at his interlocked fingers. 'Yeah, I know.'

'Will you bring her in to see me?'

'Carol's coming in to see you later. She said she'll bring her.'

At this information relief spiralled through her being, causing her to relax, her spirits to lift. 'You don't look as worse for wear as I thought you would after your binge last night,' she commented.

A glimmer of a smile played over his lips and as his blue eyes lifted to hers she was deeply shocked to realise that a long time had passed by since she had seen them twinkling with laughter and alight with mischief as they had been in New Zealand, or even on Maui . . .

'My tolerance for the stuff isn't as high as it used to be and consequently it doesn't take as much as it did to put me under,' he told her.

'Where did you go?'

'To Chinatown.'

Gina's eyes on him locked suddenly with his. 'To Mi-Ling's?' she heard herself ask.

'I was with Mi-Ling, yes.'

Gina didn't know why this admission should cause her throat to feel as though it was constricting so completely, so utterly that it would never be prised open again. 'Who is she, Mitch?' she managed to ask, her voice issuing huskily from a source of excruciating pain and forcing up past the obstruction in her throat.

'She's a lady I know.'

'Is—is she a—prostitute?'

Mitch's eyes became like granite. 'She's a lady,' he repeated, a certain emotion in his voice that Gina had never heard before. 'One of the most special women I

know. It was she who found you and rang for an
ambulance. She saw you walking about like some
mindless tourist and decided, for my sake, to keep an
eye on you until you were out of the district. Whether
or not it was because she arrived on the scene that the
thug didn't stick his knife into you, I guess we'll never
know, but it's not the first favour she's done me—and
the boys in my Company. Not by a long shot!'

Gina stared at him helplessly, while her bewilderment
grew to agonising proportions. 'I don't understand,
Mitch—the way of life here or the people. Half of the
time I don't even seem to recognise the language. It's as
if I've entered a whole new world, but I promise you I
didn't deliberately ignore your wishes. I was careless, I
suppose, and wandered for hours without paying
much attention to where I was going. Don't you
believe me?' she asked when he sat motionlessly
staring at her, appearing to be quite unmoved by her
explanation.

Expelling a short deep sigh, Mitch stood up and
returned the chair to its proper place. 'Sure, I believe
you,' he said, the expression in the gaze upon her more
remote than she'd ever seen it. 'Just as I believe you're
too indifferent towards me to deliberately ignore or
consciously heed much of anything I might have to
request of or say to you.'

'That's not so!' Gina protested on a partially audible
gasp. But there came no response, for Mitch had taken
his leave even before she had finished speaking.

CHAPTER TEN

IT was Carol who arrived to call for her the day she
was discharged, and although she chatted brightly to
her throughout the drive home, Gina sensed on several
occasions that she had opened her mouth to give voice
to something rather profound in content but spoke
instead of something quite trivial. Had Gina herself not

been as taken up as she was with the concern she was feeling over the change and the increased cooling in Mitch's attitude towards her, she might have tentatively enquired of Carol if there was something on her mind she was wishing to discuss with her.

When, upon their arrival, Carol insisted on assisting her with her belongings Gina was both grateful and yet disquieted. She felt in dire need of some form of support during the initial stages of her homecoming, but at the same time had no wish for Carol to be a witness to the strained greeting between herself and Mitch which she knew for certain would ensue.

It was Kim-Lan who unwittingly saved the day, and Gina was not so much relieved as genuinely over-whelmed with joy when the dainty child slithered down from the table where she had been sitting beside Mitch, cutting and pasting pictures from a magazine into a scrapbook, and raced past him towards her, the straight pigtails caught above her ears bobbing and her piquant face alight, crying: 'Gi—na, Gi—na!'

All Gina was conscious of was the falling away from her of the intolerable burden forced upon her by the worry that her separation from the child might rob her of the confidence she had worked so long and sedulously to gain during the months before her misadventure. In place of the weight that had rolled away came an almost euphoric sense of well-being, and she found herself laughing as she crouched to catch the child, so small and fragile, and swing her up and around in her arms.

It was quite by accident that, as she whirled and straightened with the child in her arms, her dancing eyes skimmed over the narrow length of mirrored glass inlaid in the wall of the sideboard. In it she glimpsed reflected the still silent figure of Mitch now situated behind her, and the expression on his face sent a wave of such violent, time-stopping shock pounding through her that her grip on Kim-Lan lessened to such an extent that the child squealed as Gina almost dropped her. She turned quickly, her arms tightening to the opposite extreme, but there was no longer a trace of emotion on his face, much less the evidence of the agony she had seen written so starkly in his eyes and carved into his features only seconds before.

She hadn't imagined it, she told herself as she thanked and bade farewell to Carol, whose uncommonly solemn manner she failed to perceive because there was no vacant place in the chaotic churning of her preoccupied thoughts.

Lou. Carol. Both of them had told her and both had been right after all. Mitch was in love with her. He actually loved her! She was filled with awe.

In the days that followed, Mitch gave her many causes to doubt the validity of this incredible discovery, but equally were the occasions when a vivid picture of him, as she had seen him in the innocent narrow strip of mirrored glass, flashed into her mind, and it was times such as these that kept her sane. Gradually, however, even that peace of mind became threatened as she grew more and more aware of what instigated it.

Days passed during which Gina seemed to function like an automaton, while Mitch seemed to become daily more and more detached. Apart from the salutatory kisses, and even they were performed perfunctorily, he appeared to want to avoid all form of contact with her, and he had not attempted to make love to her at all since her return from hospital.

At first this did not alarm her. On the contrary, she was unutterably thankful. One thing she needed more than anything else at this juncture was time, time to think and to assess the effect that this new turn of events was going to have over their relationship, for surely they couldn't go on as they were, and time to meditate and delve into her own feelings.

She didn't much care for the latter exercise. To take the dustcover off her own feelings and bare her soul, no matter how privately, to the cold light of day, light which was all-revealing, ruthless and uncomplimentary, would eventually expose a full true picture of herself as she really was, and this, she knew, would prove to be not a very pretty sight.

She never professed to be one who loved her fellow

man, for she had allowed the actions of one, so
unworthy, so pitiful, to dissuade her from loving
anyone, ever again. Then someone had arrived on the
scene with the key to her imprisoned inactive capacity
to love. A tiny innocent, totally dependent creature who
would, without investment of risk on her part, respond
to love as naturally as a newborn calf to its mother's
milk, and love unconditionally in return—for who, at
three, had learned the art of deceit and treachery? To
love Kim-Lan had posed no threat whatsoever.

Whereas to love Mitch ... Gina became aware, as
she often did these days, that she was gazing at him in a
fixed, rather trance-like fashion as he ate the evening
meal which she had, as she found herself doing more
often lately, gone to a great deal of trouble to prepare.
Whereas to love Mitch had been unthinkable. Mitch,
who had at first appeared as a clod to her, so big, so
earthy, so unconventional, with an animal-like energy
and passion in and for all he did, coupled with an
inordinate lust for life and laughter. This was the Mitch
she had disparaged and yet had become caught
unawares and carried away by a desire for him which
she had been unable to understand. How ashamed she
would have been, she had often thought during those
first few months of marriage, if she had not seen the
reflection of her own desire in his eyes as they rested
upon her. If this hadn't been so, she would never have
been able to accept the shamefulness of a life lived with
a man who signified all she disapproved of in a man
and with whom shared passion was their only common
ground. But at least he didn't love her, she had thought.
Nor she him. In which case neither had a responsibility
towards the other, which would be too awesome, for
her at least, to accept. And neither had a weapon with
which to bring into force against the other.

How it had suited her to see him in the light she had
and to overlook his tenderness, his humour, his
solicitous concern for her welfare and ignore the
glimpses she had had of some nameless force locked
deep within him, like vast quantities of water behind
floodgates waiting to be unleashed. All along she had

been given cause to suspect that he was capable of a depth of compassion and gentleness, but she had steadfastly refused to acknowledge or dwell upon it. If he was capable of depth and yearned to love, a target which as far as she could see had only to be herself, she didn't want to know, because she accepted without question that she would never be able to meet him. And the more she had come to know him, the more she discovered she had to learn and the more convinced of her inadequacy she became.

Mitch knew too much, about the world, about men and women, about life and suffering—too much about everything. In comparison she knew nothing—never would know anything. It was as if he had come, not only from another country, culture and background but another world, another time, and these periodic insights into the facets which made up the whole man had frightened her. He had been too hurt for words to describe adequately. He had experienced and seen that which was unspeakable. He had never been loved by parents and nor, it seemed, had he had a boyhood, but had always had to be a man. Memories of his past life had always been something not to be cherished but to be forgotten, except that he owned a subconscious that plagued and would not obey him. And yet, in spite of it all, such a man loved her, the proud, phoney Gina Wells, the empty shallow self-pitying creature who had looked upon him as a thorn in her side of which she couldn't be rid, and who had spurned, ridiculed and despised him. Where had she come by the gall?

At that moment in her musings and newly acquired humility, Mitch rose abruptly to his feet and, as he often did these evenings, announced that he was going out, and promptly did so.

On such nights, with Kim-Lan asleep in bed and the house, more quiet it seemed than her own had ever been, she would sit curled up on the sofa beneath the corner lamp and try to concentrate on her sewing or her sketching of the dresses she had visions of eventually making for Kim-Lan. However, as Mitch began to spend less and less of his free time at home, Gina found it increasingly impossible to allot even scant attention to a light television programme, much less to any of her hobbies which required her full powers of concentration.

She had to do something, she knew. But what? Whatever it was he did when he was out, she was able to discern that a certain amount of drinking was involved. He never came home even slightly drunk, that she could tell, but the amount he did consume certainly seemed to ensure that he fell swiftly into a deep, if sometimes, troubled sleep.

When her mind began to delight in torturing her more and more with pictures of him in the company of the warm and womanly Mi-Ling, she knew in a sudden fit of desperation that she intended to keep him and that there was nothing she wouldn't do to make certain she did.

On arriving at this decision, she felt fired with a new strength and sense of purpose. But to her dismay she found her bravado waning to the point of desertion that evening when, after having been home for less than an hour, Mitch made the announcement she had expected to hear after, but definitely not before, dinner. Determined however to at least make the attempt to assert herself, Gina followed him slowly to their room and stood, leaning a little on the door jamb for support, and watched him change out of his shirt. Trembling from head to foot, she stared, her face taut with apprehension and indecision. Almost four weeks had ensued since the breakdown of communication between them, and it occurred to her that she had left it too late, far too late, to take this stand. She had no idea how to begin or what to say.

As it happened, she wasn't called upon to take the initiative, because Mitch rounded on her without warning, awarding her the full benefit of a wild, brilliant-eyed look of precariously contained anger—agonised anger.

In an instant every vestige of blood fled from her face, leaving her skin cold and clammy as though touched by the very fingers of death. Even her heart seemed to have stopped dead with fear, causing her breath to diminish and her breathing to become laboured.

'Will you stop trying to get inside my head, goddammit!' he exploded, raising his voice to her as he had never done before. 'Stop watching me and trying to read my every thought and action. Leave a man some privacy, some pride, for Pete's sake!'

'I—Mitch.' She ran her tongue over suddenly dry lips and desperately grappled with courage that was beating a rapid retreat. 'I—I think we ought to talk, don't you? I really don't want you to go out tonight. Please, please stay home and let's talk.' Becoming aware that he was eyeing contemptuously the hands she was unconsciously extending to him in supplication, she dropped them and wiped them along the side seams of her beige slacks.

'Talk?' he asked, now looking at her insinuatively.

Her cheeks burned as he succeeded in his aim to humiliate her. 'Do you . . .?' she swallowed painfully but struggled on in a low voice: 'Do you wish you hadn't—married me?'

After a short silence, Mitch laughed grimly, taking off his clean shirt and pulling off the undershirt he had overlooked changing. 'I might sure as hell wish I'd never set eyes on you, but I certainly don't wish I'd never married you. I think it may be the other way around.'

'No! How can you think that? What reason have I given you to think it?'

'Sorry.' He sorted through his drawers, his movements abrupt with suppressed violence. 'I was forgetting that if you hadn't married me you'd never have fallen in love again, would you? With Lan. A nice safe cosy little affair to indulge in. No demands, no threats.' He rammed the drawer shut and jerked open another. 'Where are all my damn undershirts?'

'Mitch!' she beseeched him, once again raising her hands, her desire this time to placate him for it frightened her witless to see him like this. 'Can't we *please* talk?'

'About what? How I've been neglecting you this past

month? Are you complaining? I'd have thought you'd be relieved to escape *my* attentions now that you've finally met someone you've found it in your atrophied capacity to love!'

Gina blanched, feeling pain as great as if he had actually hit her in the region of her heart. Doggedly, she ignored the pain and pressed on: 'I know I've been putting Lan first, and I'm sorry.' She gestured in frustration as he pulled on a clean undershirt and reached for his shirt, all the while surveying her with unveiled cynicism. 'How can I make you believe me?'

'If you were even half a woman, you'd work that one out,' he told her, displaying more cruelty than she would have ever thought him capable of. It glittered in his eyes and had marred his face, causing her to fall back in shock. Was this how he looked, was this the expression he had unconsciously perfected in Vietnam when in combat with the enemy?

'I don't—understand you,' she said, her voice cracked and wavering. He sighed and tucked in his shirt. 'Yeah, I know.'

'But I want to—really, I do. I want to put right all that's gone wrong between us. Did my wandering into Chinatown start it?' she persisted frantically. 'I didn't go there deliberately. I told you that and it's the truth. I wouldn't go behind your back to do anything.'

Mitch was expressionless as he dropped his used clothing into the laundry receptacle.

'If it's Lan then I've told you. I realise how thoughtless I've been and I will put you first in future, I promise.'

Without a word he brushed past her into the hall.

'Well, at least tell me where you prefer to be if it's not here,' she said dully, going limp as she faced defeat.

He turned, saying obliquely: 'Preference has nothing to do with it.' Quite suddenly his expression became pent and he said: 'All I know for sure is that if I stayed here I'd do something I'd regret.'

'Like throttle me,' was all Gina could surmise that to mean, and all at once anger surged through her, making her reckless. 'Is it to Mi-Ling's you go?' she asked as again he turned his back on her.

He swung round, his eyes glinting with a dark malevolent humour. 'I've work to catch up on. Work that I can do now because every piece of paper I look at no longer has your face inscribed upon it. Then I go and have a drink with the guys before I come home. It makes the nights more tolerable if I can sleep. But when you see me shower before I go out,' he mocked her, 'then you'll have cause to suspect me of consorting with another woman.'

At this, Gina's ears seemed to ring and everything within her range of vision became distant. 'If you ever cheat on me,' she heard herself threaten, her voice shaking, 'I'll make sure you rue more than the day you met me!'

'More than I do now?' he asked quietly, taking a menacing step towards her.

But anger endued her with a rather nebulous form of bravery, enabling her to meet his gaze full on, her own diamond-bright and as feline as a provoked cat ready to strike. 'I'll never let you go, Mitch—I promise you that.' By her sides her hands curled into fists. 'I never fought my sister when she took Norrie away from me, but I'll fight tooth and nail to keep you, I swear it.'

Something leapt within the dark inky brilliance of his eyes. Gina didn't know what it was and she was too beside herself to care. 'Why? Why would you do that?' he asked, his voice containing the unlikely blend of both sandpaper and silk. 'Tell me why, Gina,' he commanded, 'and don't drive me to do that something I'll regret!'

Her bravado had crumbled in an instant and her head had bowed, but no sooner had her chin lowered than Mitch's hand was under it, impelling it none too gently to rise and, with courage that had to come from a source that was less ephemeral than anger, Gina lifted her eyes to his. 'I—I don't want to lose you,' she stumbled. 'I never want to lose you,' she reiterated. She gestured. 'How is the best way to tell you how much I need you? How I've grown to admire and appreciate you, your honesty and directness, your warmth and tenderness . . .' His hand dropped away from her chin and she saw the new life in his eyes die just before he turned abruptly away. 'Mitch, please don't turn away from me!' She touched his arm. 'I couldn't bear to go through another four weeks like the last, or even another six months like the last six months. I think you loved me once, don't let it be too late. Please love me again, and let me show you how much I love you.' He stiffened as though with shock. 'Mitch, I love you so.' She encircled his upper arm in her hands and pressed her face against the steely strength of it, murmuring soft her plea. 'Please, let's start again.'

With a smothered imprecation he tore himself free, took her arms in a vice-like grip and shook her with restrained violence. 'My God, if you're playing with me ...'

'I'm not!' Gina cried, white to her lips. 'Mitch, you're hurting me!'

'I'd like to wring your damn neck for what you've done to me!' he ground out. Then, holding her firmly against him with one hand, he lifted the other to grip her hair. Jerking back her head, he took what seemed an eternity but what was in effect only a second to scan her fear-filled eyes and ashen face before lowering his head to almost brand her neck with his kisses. When his lips sought hers it was with a groan. The gut sound sent a thrill stabbing through her which ended abruptly when he drew her lips between his teeth. For some time he seemed intent on inflicting upon her alternately both pain and ecstasy and, as though something within her was witnessing to her his need to punish her for the torment he had suffered, she submitted mutely until his anger was spent and his kisses became those of a man who loved her with a depth she had never dreamed of. His lips adored her, exhorted and coaxed her, and tutored her in ways she had never experienced in all the months of her marriage, and, awed by the realisation of what she had missed, she was eager to respond to his demands, both silent and spoken, lost as she had never been before in an all-consuming desire to please a man.

'Mitch ...' Her murmurings became suddenly more intelligible, more vocal. 'Mitch ...'

'No!' The husky quality of voice was in direct variance with the explosiveness of his negative response. He laughed suddenly, but darkness had fallen and she was unable to see his face. 'Not this time, sweetheart.' The endearment was lovingly spoken. 'You have my full permission to seduce me after dinner, but this time you and I are definitely going out to dine.' And he put her firmly away from him.

'But what about Kim-Lan?'

'I'll ring and ask Carol to come over for a few hours.'

'You can't do that!'

'I can, and I know she'll be delighted to do us this favour. Now, while I make the necessary phone calls,' he switched on the dressing table lamp, 'you make yourself ready.'

Once seated at their table in the dining-room of the Royal Hawaiian which looked out over a palm-lined, torchlit Waikiki beach, Gina wondered with a smile why Mitch had brought her to this plush exotic setting when all her attempts to appreciate their surroundings failed and, like pins to a magnet, her eyes found their way back to the face of her beloved, more relaxed than she had seen it for a long time.

She had long ceased to find him 'ugly', for over the months she had unconsciously grown to accept that he had far too much integrity and character which gave beauty to features that were a team made up of good and bad. It was a broad face, with a nose as aggressively moulded as his jaw, and thick straight brows over eyes that were deep-set, vital, always extraordinarily alive and communicative. But how long had they hidden the love he felt for her or, perhaps more importantly, how long had she been tragically blind to the love written there and displayed in the shape of his wide expressive mouth? So, filled with remorse and mortification, she wanted to reach forth a hand and cradle his cheek and convey to him her contrition by pressing her lips reverently to each dear and unique feature, ugly, beautiful, both. But their surroundings were by no stretch of the imagination private, and in the grip of irritation she suddenly became aware that Mitch was watching her watch him. His eyes held hers and their depths appeared to be ablaze.

'If you persist in sitting there looking at me like that,' he warned softly, 'I'm not going to be responsible for my actions!'

'I don't know what we're doing here at all,' Gina teased lightly, while at the same time fighting for equilibrium. 'The last thing we need is an audience.'

'Later, I promise we'll find ourselves some lonely remote spot, a moonlit bay . . . Well, well, you're blushing! More now than you did on our honeymoon. Don't tell me you've forgotten already all the deserted beaches we stumbled across, sunlit as well as moonlit?'

'No, of course not!' Flustered, she averted her gaze. 'But I wasn't in love then . . .'

'And you're afraid of loving me, is that it? Look at me, Gina.'

'I suppose I am just a little,' Gina admitted, tearing her eyes away from the mesmerising flicker of a fire torch to meet his.

'I'd say more than just a little!'

'Perhaps. But I wouldn't change the way I feel for you even if I could. Nor would I exchange tonight for any other night of our marriage. I just wish I'd discovered earlier how I felt or how you felt.'

'When did you discover how I felt?' he asked.

Gina told him. 'If you loved me why didn't you tell me?'

'When should I have told you?'

She shrugged helplessly. 'Wouldn't when you discovered you did have been the appropriate time?'

Mitch grimaced wryly. 'I never made such a discovery.'

Gina looked at him blankly, then remembered with dawning horror that he had never actually made a declaration of love to her. She had caught a glimpse of a single fleeting expression on his face and had placed upon it, and accepted without question, her own interpretation of it. 'Do you mean that—that I'm assuming too much. You—you don't love me?' she whispered.

'What I mean is that there was never a moment when I didn't. I simply always knew I did.'

'Since—since when?'

'Since the moment I picked up your scattered groceries and looked into a pair of rather dazed and definitely troubled grey-green eyes. I was ensnared utterly, for it was then that I first realised that part of myself, a graft, had been missing, and suddenly I'd found it and I knew immediately that the freedom I had cherished was, and had always been, nothing more than a myth I'd clung to in vain. She, I thought, I was born for, formed for, and I'd die for her.'

Each word, precious and beautiful though they were, fell upon her like a blow and with each word she was struck numb, dumb and blind. She groped, to find her feet, her serviette, the edge of the table and finally, the strength she needed to transport herself out of that dining-room, which had become more and more an arena to her, in which they at their table were the central fixture, the main attraction.

Sand swallowed her sandals and sucked at her feet until finally she kicked off the sandals, scooped them up, and ran along the edge of gently lapping moonlit water until, a short time later, her progress was further impeded by a clasping of her arm.

'Gina! For God's sake, what's wrong? What did I say?' Having caught her, Mitch spun her around and the impetus of her flight brought her against him with such force, they both staggered and the sandals fell from her hands. 'Gina!' He righted them and gazed down into her tear-wet face. 'What's wrong? What did I say?'

'H—how could you have?' she cried. 'How could you have?' She pummelled his chest weakly with bunched fists and sobbed: 'I was—I was just so—so awful! It can't possibly be true. It's not fair of you.'

'Gina . . .'

'Tell me it's not true, that you're making it up.'

'I can't, Gina . . . For Pete's sake, will you quit

struggling and quieten down!' Abruptly, she heeded him and sank, shuddering, against him. 'That's better,' he spoke soothingly, burying his lips in her hair, murmuring endearments, his hands, square and capable, tightening on her body, imparting to her some of their assurance.

'I'm so ashamed,' she whispered as his lips tenderly gathered her tears.

'No, no . . .'

She drew back, staunchly resisting his efforts to mollify her. 'I was a beast to you. I had a chip on my shoulder the size of a house, and I took it out on you. I despised you and shunned you. How could you possibly have loved me when I was so foul and behaved so abominably?'

She felt gentle laughter quiver through him and she looked up at him and obligingly he explained: 'Don't you think I saw through all that and saw you as I knew you could be? You, as you really were, lurked somewhere underneath that self-cultivated sham, and it irked me to realise that I would have to impose a curb on myself and work my way through it chipping the layers away. I knew then how a diamond cutter must feel, waiting for a gem of finest quality to emerge. Patience certainly is a virtue and sometimes acquired by men, and determination I've always had. I couldn't help but win.'

Gina listened and she stared at him spellbound. 'I never knew,' she spoke as if to herself. 'You never told me, never gave me an inkling. Not once.'

'And if I had told you, what would I have achieved? Precisely nothing. As for inklings, I gave you many. I tried to show you a thousand different ways. I tried to tell you in all my actions—the evidence was there, but you never saw it and I knew I had to wait until the time came when you wanted to see it. The hell of it was the waiting. I thought the time would never come.' He reached for her and drew her into the haven of his arms and Gina brought down his head and caught fully the wide curve of his lips with her own, eager to begin to make amends, and for them, time and matter ceased to have any relevance.

'So many months,' her aching whisper glanced across the corner of his mouth. 'Wasted. And I can't atone—not for them or for the ways I've hurt you.'

'Nothing's wasted. There were times when I enjoyed the chase and enjoyed the fight, and the prize was certainly worth it!'

She pressed her mouth to his, murmuring later, 'Let's go home.'

'Uh-uh.' Mitch put her slightly but firmly away from him, dropping a kiss on her nose to allay the pain of what he could see she took to be his rejection of her. He gathered up her sandals. 'Bodies have a tendency to get in the way—which is perfectly agreeable under most circumstances, but it's not every day that my wife tells me for the first time that she loves me. I want to be with you, like this, strolling arm in arm along Waikiki Beach. Okay?'

'I suppose so,' and laughing, tasting tentatively her newfound happiness, Gina slipped both her arms about him as they began to walk and responded in kind: 'After all, it's not every day that you display your true colours either. So romantic, who would have guessed? And a poet too.' She fell into a thoughtful silence. Then, humbly, she buried her face against his side, kissing him through his light jacket.

His arm tightened about her. 'I never thought the day would dawn when I'd say I liked this beach, but,' his head went back and he laughed aloud, 'I think right now there's not one in the world I like better.'

'Not even Himatangi?' Gina teased, looking up at him guilessly.

'Ah, that brings me to another subject that's been on my mind during these last few weeks. I received a letter from your father when you were in hospital.'

Gina stopped still in surprise. 'You did? And never told me . . .' she stiffened as another thought struck her. 'There's nothing wrong, is there?'

'No, no.' Mitch gave her a tug and they began walking once more. 'He's had the offer of a small kiwi fruit farm in the district and has decided to buy it.'

'Without telling me?'

'Simply because at this stage it has more to do with

me than you. He's going to have to put Tiraumea on the market and wants me to know if I'd like first option.'

'What!' Gina gasped. 'Are you serious?'

'Never more so.'

'Do you mean to say you've been sitting on news like this for four weeks! Why didn't you mention this before?'

'Because, dammit, I didn't know how to bring it up. Things between us were deteriorating so rapidly, I didn't know what to do for the best.'

'And now? What do you propose to do now?'

'You have a say in that. Only if we stay here and I stay in the Army, I can never become an officer—not even for you.'

'I never wanted you to become an officer. That was a product of your over-active imagination, that one. All I want is for you to do whatever you're happiest doing.'

'You like Tiraumea, don't you?'

'Of course. It was my home. I love every nail, every board of totara in it.'

'Then you wouldn't mind exchanging Paradise for Tiraumea.'

'*Mitch!*' Gina stopped, and her breath stopped, while Mitch walked on a further few steps before pausing to look back at her, somewhat diffidently. 'Do you mean it? Do you really mean it?' Laughter, joyous and excited, bubbled up and over. She flew into his arms and flinging her own about him, swung on his neck. 'If you mean would I exchange Purgatory for Paradise— you can bet I would! But are you sure?' she probed, serious all at once. She lowered her feet to the sand and looked at him anxiously. 'Isn't it a gamble?'

'I've learned to thrive on gambles,' he told her, grinning significantly and running one crooked fore-finger down the line of her nose. 'And taking into account my determination, how can I lose?'

'Oh, Mitch!' Gina felt aglow. She hadn't known it was possible to be so happy.

'Besides which, Kim-Lan will flourish more healthily there. It will be a good life for her and a good environment for us to bring up our children.'

Lifting her face, Gina pressed a lingering kiss against the side of his cheek and held him tightly until, in silence, they resumed their walk.

'Kim-Lan's not my child,' he spoke at length, and Gina's heart bounded in an expression of both peace and gladness, not in response to the content of his disclosure but because at last he wanted to talk to her about the things which concerned him. Kim-Lan, she knew, was only the beginning. 'She's the daughter of a close friend of mine—Eddie was the best pal I ever had . . .'

And because his arm didn't return to its position around her, she re-established contact between them by slipping both hers through one of his, loving this man who had finally become to her, so precious, a man above all men.

A wonderful **new** service
from **Mills & Boon**

Your very own
Horoscope

ONLY £5

Discover the real you

Mills & Boon are offering you this special chance to discover what it is that makes you tick — your emotions — your strengths — your weaknesses and how you appear to others.

A 6,000 word horoscope will be prepared for you using the latest computer techniques. The interpretation is written under the guidance of the UK's leading astrologers.

For just £5.00 you will receive
- A full birth chart
- A list of planetary aspects
- A detailed 6,000 word character analysis
- A monthly forecast of your year ahead **or** — for an extra £3.50 — a forecast of the principle trends for the next ten years.

. . . all beautifully bound and presented in an attractive lilac folder.

The perfect gift!

Simply fill in the coupon below and send it with your cheque or postal order made payable to 'Horoscope Offer', P.O. Box 20, Tunbridge Wells, Kent TN4 9NP.
Please allow 28 days for delivery.

TO: MILLS & BOON HOROSCOPE SERVICE   8HS
PLEASE USE BLOCK CAPITALS

NAME: MR/MRS/MISS . . . .

ADDRESS . . . .

. . . .

My birth information is:
Place . . . . County . . . .

Country . . . . Date . . . . . . Time . . . . am/pm
              (If time unknown we will use midday)

Please send me . . . . qty)

1 year horoscope at £5.00   **Overseas**
10 year horoscope at £8.50   Add £1.00 extra for
I enclose cheque/P.O. for £ . . . .   postage and packing

An orchestra for you

In the Rose of Romance Orchestra, conducted by Jack Dorsey of '101 Strings' fame, top musicians have been brought together especially to reproduce in music the moods and sounds of Romance.

The Rose of Romance Orchestra brings you classic romantic songs like Yours, Just the Way You Are, September Song and many others.

We promise you a new dimension of pleasure and enjoyment as you read your favourite romances from Mills & Boon.

Volumes 1 & 2 now available on the Rose Records label wherever good records are bought.

Usual price £3.99 (Record or Cassette)

Mills & Boon

The rose of romance.

How to join in a whole new world of romance

It's very easy to subscribe to the Mills & Boon Reader Service. As a regular reader, you can enjoy a whole range of special benefits. Bargain offers. Big cash savings. Your own free Reader Service newsletter, packed with knitting patterns, recipes, competitions, and exclusive book offers.

We send you the very latest titles each month, postage and packing free – no hidden extra charges. There's absolutely no commitment – you receive books for only as long as you want.

We'll send you details. Simply send the coupon – or drop us a line for details about the Mills & Boon Reader Service Subscription Scheme. Post to: Mills & Boon Reader Service, P.O. Box 236, Thornton Road, Croydon, Surrey CR9 3RU, England. *Please note: READERS IN SOUTH AFRICA please write to: Mills & Boon Reader Service of Southern Africa, Private Bag X3010, Randburg 2125, S. Africa.

Please send me details of the Mills & Boon Subscription Scheme.

NAME (Mrs/Miss) _____ EP3

ADDRESS _____

_____

COUNTY/COUNTRY_____ POST/ZIP CODE _____

BLOCK LETTERS, PLEASE

Mills & Boon
the rose of romance